Taken With You

Also From Carrie Ann Ryan

The Montgomery Ink: Boulder Series:
Book 1: *Wrapped in Ink*
Book 2: *Sated in Ink*
Book 3: *Embraced in Ink*
Book 4: *Seduced in Ink*
Book 4.5: *Captured in Ink*

The Montgomery Ink: Fort Collins Series:
Book 1: *Inked Persuasion*

The Less Than Series:
Book 1: *Breathless With Her*
Book 2: *Reckless With You*
Book 3: *Shameless With Him*

The Elements of Five Series:
Book 1: *From Breath and Ruin*
Book 2: *From Flame and Ash*
Book 3: *From Spirit and Binding*
Book 4: *From Shadow and Silence*

The Promise Me Series:
Book 1: *Forever Only Once*
Book 2: *From That Moment*
Book 3: *Far From Destined*
Book 4: *From Our First*

The Fractured Connections Series:
Book 1: *Breaking Without You*
Book 2: *Shouldn't Have You*
Book 3: *Falling With You*
Book 4: *Taken With You*

Montgomery Ink: Colorado Springs
Book 1: *Fallen Ink*
Book 2: *Restless Ink*
Book 2.5: *Ashes to Ink*

Book 4: *Wolf Betrayed*
Book 5: *Fractured Silence*
Book 6: *Destiny Disgraced*
Book 7: *Eternal Mourning*
Book 8: *Strength Enduring*
Book 9: *Forever Broken*

Redwood Pack Series
Book 1: *An Alpha's Path*
Book 2: *A Taste for a Mate*
Book 3: *Trinity Bound*
Book 3.5: *A Night Away*
Book 4: *Enforcer's Redemption*
Book 4.5: *Blurred Expectations*
Book 4.7: *Forgiveness*
Book 5: *Shattered Emotions*
Book 6: *Hidden Destiny*
Book 6.5: *A Beta's Haven*
Book 7: *Fighting Fate*
Book 7.5: *Loving the Omega*
Book 7.7: *The Hunted Heart*
Book 8: *Wicked Wolf*

Branded Packs (Written with Alexandra Ivy)
Book 1: *Stolen and Forgiven*
Book 2: *Abandoned and Unseen*
Book 3: *Buried and Shadowed*

Dante's Circle Series
Book 1: *Dust of My Wings*
Book 2: *Her Warriors' Three Wishes*
Book 3: *An Unlucky Moon*
Book 3.5: *His Choice*
Book 4: *Tangled Innocence*
Book 5: *Fierce Enchantment*
Book 6: *An Immortal's Song*
Book 7: *Prowled Darkness*
Book 8: *Dante's Circle Reborn*

Holiday, Montana Series
Book 1: *Charmed Spirits*
Book 2: *Santa's Executive*
Book 3: *Finding Abigail*
Book 4: *Her Lucky Love*
Book 5: *Dreams of Ivory*

The Happy Ever After Series:
Flame and Ink
Ink Ever After

Single Title:
Finally Found You

Taken With You

A Fractured Connections Novella

By Carrie Ann Ryan

1001 DARK NIGHTS
PRESS

Taken With You
A Fractured Connections Novella
By Carrie Ann Ryan

1001 Dark Nights

Copyright 2020 Carrie Ann Ryan
ISBN: 978-1-970077-42-1

Foreword: Copyright 2014 M. J. Rose

Cover photo credit © Annie Ray/ Passion Pages

Published by 1001 Dark Nights Press, an imprint of Evil Eye Concepts,
Incorporated

Acknowledgments from the Author

The Fractured Connections series is one of my more emotional series, so being able to write about two characters who find their happiness even in the darkness was important to me. I wouldn't have been able to write this romance without 1,001 Dark Nights and I'm forever grateful that I was given the opportunity to write about second chances when all seems lost.

I want to thank Liz, MJ, and Jillian for creating such an amazing family that I get to be part of where so many people are connected and uplifted by writing and working with the one thing we all adore: The HEA.

Thank you as well to my BFF and editor, Chelle, for making sure I stayed on target when I really wanted to explore more of my hero's background. (And I just might anyway!)

As always, thank you dear readers for staying with me throughout the years. I can't wait to see where we go!

Sign up for the 1001 Dark Nights Newsletter
and be entered to win a Tiffany Key necklace.

There's a contest every month!

Go to www.1001DarkNights.com to subscribe.

**As a bonus, all subscribers can download
FIVE FREE exclusive books!**

One Thousand and One Dark Nights

Once upon a time, in the future…

*I was a student fascinated with stories and learning.
I studied philosophy, poetry, history, the occult, and
the art and science of love and magic. I had a vast
library at my father's home and collected thousands
of volumes of fantastic tales.*

*I learned all about ancient races and bygone
times. About myths and legends and dreams of all
people through the millennium. And the more I read
the stronger my imagination grew until I discovered
that I was able to travel into the stories… to actually
become part of them.*

*I wish I could say that I listened to my teacher
and respected my gift, as I ought to have. If I had, I
would not be telling you this tale now.
But I was foolhardy and confused, showing off
with bravery.*

*One afternoon, curious about the myth of the
Arabian Nights, I traveled back to ancient Persia to
see for myself if it was true that every day Shahryar
(Persian: شهریار, "king") married a new virgin, and then
sent yesterday's wife to be beheaded. It was written
and I had read that by the time he met Scheherazade,
the vizier's daughter, he'd killed one thousand
women.*

Something went wrong with my efforts. I arrived in the midst of the story and somehow exchanged places with Scheherazade – a phenomena that had never occurred before and that still to this day, I cannot explain.

Now I am trapped in that ancient past. I have taken on Scheherazade's life and the only way I can protect myself and stay alive is to do what she did to protect herself and stay alive.

Every night the King calls for me and listens as I spin tales. And when the evening ends and dawn breaks, I stop at a point that leaves him breathless and yearning for more. And so the King spares my life for one more day, so that he might hear the rest of my dark tale.

As soon as I finish a story... I begin a new one... like the one that you, dear reader, have before you now.

Chapter 1

Beckham

"You are the person of my heart. The woman of my dreams. The other half of my soul. I'll never forget why you are mine. And why I am yours. I will do whatever is within my power to make sure that you know I'll always love you with every ounce of my being. To the last breath in my body. I love you, Harmony. With everything that I am. Be mine. Forever."

"I love you, Brendon. With every ounce of my soul, with every breath of my being. I hope that one day I will be able to really make you understand exactly how much, and how honored I am to call you mine. We walked through the darkness, and I know that even though we weren't alone, we were there for each other for a reason. And I will never regret that. You are mine, Brendon Connolly. Forever and always. And I cannot wait to see what's next."

I leaned back in my chair and just smiled up at the couple as Brendon and Harmony continued their vows in front of each other and the rest of the wedding guests. We were family in a way, friends in so many more. And I was glad that I was here, even if I'd almost stayed away. After all, I was good at being on the periphery these days. I wasn't very good at being in the middle of things.

I had been to a few weddings in my time, but never one quite like this. I didn't think there would *ever* be one quite like this.

I'd known Brendon Connolly for a few years—off and on in the past. Then a lot better recently. Particularly when he and his brothers came to take over the bar that I worked at to try and make it better. To make it a home again. I had been there for the guy. Just like I had been there for his brothers, Aiden and Cameron, as they attempted to figure out how to make their world make sense after losing their parents and coming back together as a family again.

It'd been interesting to watch them create relationships and then fall in love even when they didn't mean to. Of course—at least, in my opinion—most people didn't *mean* to fall in love. It just happened.

Not that I'd ever actually been in love. Not my thing. It was safer to not form those connections. They only left you fractured in the end.

I resisted the urge to look across the aisle at the bride's side. At *her*. There would only be pain and heartache there.

"You may now kiss your bride," the woman officiating said. Brendon dipped Harmony low, his mouth fastening to hers in a deep kiss that had the rest of the wedding guests on their feet, hooting and hollering and clapping.

I shook my head, standing up with the rest of them as I cheered as well. Then I put my fingers between my lips and whistled, a high, sharp sound that garnered a few looks.

Including hers.

I really should not be thinking about her. Or noticing her.

Though it was hard not to. Especially since she was always...there.

Not in a bad way. She was part of our new circle. The one I hadn't acknowledged I'd become a part of until I was sitting next to all the Connolly brothers and their women and suddenly realized I was one of them.

Meadow Brown was the same way, just on the opposite side of the connection line.

It was odd to think that, after all these years, I was in the same circle as she—even though I didn't think she actually knew who I was. Beyond being the bartender and the one who liked to give Brendon shit about his drink-slinging skills anyway.

I was the one with the smiles. The jokes. And that was the image I tried for. I didn't want them to know who I had been before. I wanted to hide the stains on my hands.

I didn't want to think about it either.

So I wasn't going to.

Instead, I pushed those thoughts from my mind, shoved Meadow out as well, and grinned as Brendon picked up his wife and carried her down the aisle.

Of course, the rest of the wedding party had to have fun, too.

Cameron grabbed his woman, Violet, throwing her over his

shoulder so she could smack him on the ass as they laughed and trekked down the runner.

Aiden tapped his back, and Sienna hopped on, her dress sliding up her thighs as she laughed hysterically, the two of them trying to outrun Cameron and Violet.

The last of the wedding party, Dillon, who was now nineteen or so if I remembered right, looked over at Adrienne, Violet's sister-in-law, and held out an arm.

Adrienne smiled, flipped her hair over her shoulders, and took his hand.

Adrienne's husband, Mace, stood on the bride's side, glaring at Dillon, though there was a smile on his face.

Dillon then reached down, slid his arm under Adrienne's knees, and hoisted her up.

Adrienne let out a shocked gasp and then laughed, blowing her husband a kiss as the teen carried her down the aisle and from the wedding area in a very gallant style.

The kid had game, even though I didn't think he was dating anyone. At least, not right now. But he knew how to romance women—even if it was all in jest. After all, I was pretty sure he had had a hand in helping each of his older brothers get and keep their women.

When and if I ever decided to enter a relationship, I'd either have to go to Dillon for help if I wanted to keep it. Or stay far away. The latter, especially if I knew that maintaining distance between myself and whomever I might be interested in would be the best thing for everyone.

After the wedding party had left, I followed the rest of the guests, nodding at a few as they smiled at me. I was the Connolly bartender. Meaning I knew a lot of people's names, even more faces, and their favorite drinks. I knew a few secrets, too, because everybody always talked to their favorite bartender. But most people didn't know me. And I was just fine with that.

I slid my hand over my clean-shaven face and frowned. I'd had a beard for as long as I could remember, but had shaved for the wedding. It was something my mother would have wanted me to do—not that I had seen or heard from her in decades. I didn't feel like myself anymore without the hair, though. It was weird to look at the man in the mirror and realize that…hey, that's me, the man under the beard. I wasn't sure I really liked it.

But it would grow back. Hopefully as fast as it had last time.

I'd already decided that I probably wouldn't shave for the rest of the weddings. All of the Connollys were getting married. Except for Dillon. That kid had a ways to go.

At least, I figured he did. I hoped he wouldn't get hitched at nineteen or whatever the hell age he was.

Brendon and Harmony were doing a buffet-style meal at the reception. That way, nobody had to sit down unless they wanted to. And that was just fine with me. I hated formal events where I had to play nice and act like I knew what I was doing.

Harmony's family came from money. And as I looked around the tent that we were under with all the waiters in black tie, and every little detail perfect, I realized it was evident if you looked hard enough.

I remembered Brendon and Harmony complaining at the bar one night that her parents wanted to go all out for the event, even though this was her second wedding, and she wanted to do something small.

Apparently, they'd compromised. The wedding wasn't huge or insane, but it was nice.

I looked over at the food. The piles of it looked amazing, hot, and were probably tasty, and I figured that I could handle this kind of nice.

Anything for my stomach was a good idea.

"Hey, you're late," Dillon said as he came up to my side, holding a small plate with something on a skewer that looked really fucking good. "They announced over the speakers that everybody could start eating. That way, nobody has to mill around. I think it's only appetizers for now. Not quite sure. Never been to one of these things." Dillon shrugged before taking a bite. The kid's eyes rolled back, and he moaned.

"Good stuff?" I asked, sliding my hands into my suit pants' pockets.

"The best. Just don't tell Aiden, because he didn't actually cook this."

I laughed and then shook my head. "But one of his friends did, right?"

"Yeah, one of the chefs that worked with him at his old place. He ended up leaving after Aiden did. The whole place is a mess now because of the owner's son or whoever ended up being the head chef. Not quite sure what the whole story is, but Aiden's friend opened up a catering business, and I think the Connollys are going to hire them. I don't mind. There's some good stuff here." Dillon took another bite and moaned again. "Seriously good stuff."

"I'll have to get some, then."

"So why were you late?" Dillon asked, taking another bite.

My mouth was watering at this point, but I figured I could talk for a bit. "I was just walking around before I came in here. I was like thirty seconds behind you, seriously." I rolled my eyes and then gestured for the kid to walk over to the buffet area with me. They had stations everywhere so, thankfully, there wasn't a huge line. I got a little plate of skewers, some cheese, and figured I'd save room for the rest of the dinner. I hadn't been hungry before, but smelling all the food? Now, I was downright famished. I looked up and met Meadow's gaze across the aisle.

Great, now I was starving for something else. The kick in my gut that always came when I saw her did its thing. I ignored it and gave her a smile, then winked and turned away. I didn't want to see her reaction.

I honest to God didn't know if she even remembered me from before. Previous to the first time she'd walked into the bar to meet with Violet. I really hoped she didn't. I didn't want that part of my past out in the world. And, from the way she acted, I had a feeling no one knew her past either.

It was better for both of us if we ignored it.

And that's what I would keep telling myself.

It wasn't as if she and I had truly talked before that first bar meeting. I'd only seen her from afar, and we'd never actually *met*.

"So you ready to move out?" I asked before taking a bite. "Hold that thought. Dear God, this is amazing."

Aiden looked over Sienna's head and glared at me.

I flipped him the bird before eating some more.

The other man just rolled his eyes, a laugh twitching his mouth before he moved his attention back to his woman. Good. That was where it was supposed to be. Not on me and the amazing skewers I was about to come over.

"Good stuff, right? As to your question, I don't know. I don't really know if I'm ready to move out. But my friends and I all want to get a place while we're in school. You know? I don't really want to stay with Cameron forever, even though I kind of do."

I nodded, understanding, even though I hadn't really had that growing up. Then again, maybe I had. I'd moved in with a group of friends when I was about Dillon's age. But they'd gotten me into a whole shitload of trouble. Stuff that I couldn't erase, even though I wanted to bury it. I'd moved in with them not for college like Dillon, but because I'd thought they were my family. Blood in and blood out and all that shit.

Jesus, I needed to get those thoughts out of my head. I'd been thinking about my past a lot lately. And I had a feeling I knew why. And that reason was currently standing on the other side of the room.

I ignored her—I had to.

"Cameron's been taking care of you forever. He's like another dad, right?"

Dillon nodded. "Yeah. Ever since Mom did her thing. I'm okay, though."

I gave him a look that said I didn't really believe him, but I knew he was better than he had been. Honestly, he was probably the steadiest of us all. That meant I needed to watch out for the kid. Anyone who was that solid usually had something to hide. And since I knew most of the kid's background—as much as he let anyone know—I had a feeling that when Dillon broke, he would need all of us. After all, I'd needed people when I cracked. Sadly, I hadn't had anyone.

I wouldn't let that happen to Dillon.

"Anyway, I'm excited to move out. It'll be nice for Cameron and Violet to have their own place. Without me killing their buzz."

"Knowing those two, I'm sure they find ways to get together without having to worry about you."

Dillon visibly shuddered, even as he grinned. "Yeah. I don't really want to think about that. But it'll be nice not having to tiptoe around if I need something to drink in the middle of the night."

"I can see how that might be a little weird. But if you ever need anything, let me know. Okay? I know you're close to your brothers now, but I'm here for you, too. Just say the word."

Dillon smiled, his eyes warming. "You're a good man, Beckham."

I wasn't good. I was anything but. There was a reason they said you had to atone for your sins. And I was working my way through that. There would never be a happy ending for me. That was something I had learned long ago. But I could at least try not to be the person I once was.

So I smiled and took a bite of my chicken before Dillon wandered off to talk to the rest of his family.

When I was finished with my appetizer, I set down my plate and went to wash my hands.

I didn't know why I was still here. I usually showed up at places and events and then left as soon as I could. But I figured it'd be good for me to at least pretend like I belonged. Not that I always felt that way.

I leaned against the wall, watching everybody dance, smile, and act like they were having a good time. When Meadow walked by, I wasn't even sure she noticed me. It took everything within me not to notice *her*. Or *try* not to. But I couldn't help it. She was always there. In my thoughts, my past. And, lately, physically right in front of me.

And so, without thinking, I reached out and grabbed her hand.

She froze, her eyes wide as she turned around. I wanted to curse at myself.

I knew where she had come from. And, in general, I knew you didn't just go around touching women like that. Especially not when I had a feeling Meadow had been through hell.

I was such a fucking asshole. I slowly let go of her fingers and slid my hand back into my pocket.

"Hey," I said, trying to sound casual. Attempting to come across as if I hadn't seen the fear in her eyes, or the way she looked as if she were about to run.

There was fight or flight for a reason, after all. And I was bigger than Meadow. So, *flight* was the logical response.

Damn it.

"Hi," Meadow said, her throat working as she swallowed. "Having fun?" she asked, her voice soft.

"Yeah. The Connollys sure know how to host a party."

"So I see. It looks like everyone is having a great time."

A voice slid out of the speakers, and we froze. "Okay, now this is where we're going to have fun on the dance floor. Before the bride and groom do their thing, they want you guys to come out. So, find the person nearest you, doesn't matter who it is, and take them out to dance. Let's make this wedding memorable."

The announcer's voice echoed in my head, and I wanted to curse. There was only one person near me. The one I shouldn't dance with. And because I knew it would be better if we didn't, because I was really good at doing what would cause the worst pain, I held out my hand.

"You want to dance?" I asked, my voice low.

Meadow looked at me then, her eyes wide, and she smiled. She had on this jeweled green dress that hugged her curves and made her look sexy as fuck.

There were a lot of attractive women here, some showing off a lot of skin, others wearing more expensive and conservative pieces.

But Meadow was the only one I couldn't keep my gaze off, and that's why I'd tried so hard not to look.

"Okay. Only because it's part of the wedding and all."

The justification wasn't necessary. The reasoning had been going through my mind as well.

I nodded and led her out to the dance floor.

I slid one arm around her, palm resting on her lower back while the other clasped her smaller hand in mine.

"I promise I'll try not to step on your toes," I said.

She raised a brow, showing me some of the fire I knew lived inside of her. "Okay, but I'm wearing high heels. I could probably hurt you more."

I looked down our bodies to her toes and saw the same jeweled green peeking out from the bottom of her dress. I swallowed hard. Huh. *Apparently, I have a thing for her feet.*

"Okay, then. I guess we'll see who hurts the other the most."

She met my gaze, and I had a feeling we both understood the double meaning of that statement. At least, partly. But I simply smiled and started to dance.

Other couples were on the dance floor with us, so I had to pull Meadow closer to my body. She wasn't pressed against it, but she was close enough that I could feel the heat of her. Every once in a while, my body brushed along the soft curves of hers.

We didn't speak because there really wasn't much to say. She always turned from me when we were around the others, and I did my best to not stare when I was around her. I didn't know why she resisted being near me, but I sure as hell knew why I did. And I didn't want to push. I was going to have this dance, and then I would get the hell out of here.

It would be better for both of us if I did.

When the song neared its end, we found ourselves at the edge of the dance floor. There were other people around, but no one I knew. The rest of my friends were on the other side of the room.

It sounded as if the music was far away. It felt as if it were only Meadow and me in the space. This was a mistake. I knew it had been from the first touch. But I couldn't help myself.

Meadow and I kept dancing, though I wasn't even sure the music was still playing. I didn't know if anyone was around us anymore at this point.

And then, because I couldn't help it, and I was the same bastard now as I'd always been, I leaned down. I brushed my lips along Meadow's—just a soft caress that meant nothing. It had to be inconsequential. But it meant everything. She let out a shocked breath, her lips parting. My tongue brushed hers, a bare whisper of a kiss. And as I pulled back, her eyes went wide.

"Hey," I said, sounding like a fool.

She blinked at me and then released my hand. I let mine fall, and she took a step back. Then another. Before I could ask Meadow what was wrong, or apologize for doing what I did, she turned on her heel and ran.

She zigzagged through the crowd of others, but no one was really paying attention to us.

I watched her go and knew I had fucked up.

I had kissed Meadow.

And though I knew it had been a mistake, the part of me that had always been an asshole was positive I would do it again in a heartbeat.

And that, most of all, made me ashamed.

Chapter 2

He's perfectly wrong for me.
~Meadow, journal entry

Meadow

To the outside world, I knew my job was possibly the most tedious one ever. To me, though? I loved it. It wasn't monotonous or tedious. No, I got to play with words, math, and science. And, somehow, fit them all together in a textbook so someone else could learn from it.

Okay, it did sound a little boring. But I couldn't help it, it was what I was good at. Other people might get to work with their hands or bake things or create fiction with words and TV and whatnot. They used their bodies, they created.

I sort of made things. I took facts and known entities and blended them all together. And I edited others.

People in school needed those textbooks. They required the information to learn. Some things you needed a teacher for, but others demanded a base. So, yes, while it may sound lackluster to some, I helped people learn. That way, they could go out into the world and be exactly who they needed to be. Not that anybody really knew I was the one behind the work. I wasn't who came to mind when they thought about their classes. I just wrote and edited the expensive thing they had to buy before they started school. The book they occasionally opened if they wanted to actually learn in class. I was the person who wrote all the words in that giant paperweight, the thing that sometimes got lost in the trunk of your car or at the bottom of your backpack because you forgot it was there.

I loved my job.

Even though my friends didn't really understand it.

But that was fine with me. I could work in my own little bubble. I didn't need to leave the house, and I could focus on what was important: helping others. And I somehow made a living while doing it.

It wasn't always easy, though I was figuring it out. And I didn't do it alone. There was always a handful of people who worked on this type of project, and we supported one another.

My job was to handle the middle ground. To take what someone wanted to write and make it work. And then edit it before it went to the next phase of editing, or the people went through all of the science problems and tried them out to make sure they actually worked.

I mostly helped with the grammar. And some of the science. My degrees were still useful, even though I didn't leave the house much.

I wasn't a complete agoraphobe, but some days, I sure felt like one.

Working from home had made it easier for me to make the friends I currently had, though.

Not that I had many, but I did have a couple of good ones now.

Violet was my neighbor. I think we initially met while I was taking out the trash. She had been all smiles, even though her eyes had been covered by dark sunglasses, and she kept rubbing her temples.

I found out later that she got terrible migraines. So over the months of us getting to know each other, I'd helped her get through them. They were so debilitating, she needed someone to come over and make sure she took her meds and had enough water and food for when she felt better. I had quickly become that person.

She had an amazing family, and they were there for her, too, but I lived the closest.

Through Violet, I had met my other friends.

We'd lost one a bit ago now, even though it felt much more recent. I hadn't known Alison well, but she'd been kind to me, and I missed her. I knew the others missed her even more. She had been such a huge part of their lives.

But Violet, Sienna, and Harmony were my friends now. And they forced me out of my comfort zone sometimes. And out of my house.

Something I honestly needed.

I wouldn't have been able to do any of that before. Couldn't have walked into a bar to smile and laugh and get to know people. I wouldn't have been able to be around their men, large guys with even bigger personalities.

The Connolly brothers were all broad and tall and tattooed and bearded. Even the one that wore suits all the time, Brendon, tended to be a little bit ragged by the time he finished his day and ended up at the brewery with the rest of us.

It still surprised me that I could even see them and not shrink away in fear. Though, in retrospect, I'd probably cowered a bit when I first met them. But, thankfully, no one had commented on it.

Although there was one person that I should probably *still* keep away from.

And he had just kissed me a few nights ago.

Beckham.

What was wrong with me?

I couldn't believe I had let him kiss me, that I had kissed him back. I shouldn't have even danced with him that night.

It had been a horrible mistake. And I couldn't let it happen again.

I knew exactly what happened when you gave in to your base desires, or when you leaned on someone and let them get close like that.

I rubbed my wrists and looked down, still seeing the bruises that were no longer there. They had faded a few years ago, and they would never be back.

No. I wouldn't let myself be that vulnerable again.

Though the marks on my skin had faded, they were still on my soul and in my heart.

I could feel them beneath my flesh as if each ache from the blows had touched my very being.

The scars were still there, evidence of my mistakes, of the person I had been and who I'd trusted when I shouldn't have.

I wouldn't—couldn't—let Beckham kiss me again.

Actually, I would do everything in my power to never be alone with him again.

I'd already made one mistake.

I didn't know if I could afford another.

I pushed those thoughts from my mind and went back to work. I had a few more hours of data to look over, and then I could spend my afternoon doing whatever I wanted. Reading, doing some Google searches. Maybe I'd take a walk. Although I didn't really know if I wanted to do that enough to leave the house.

The four walls and roof that surrounded me seemed like my only salvation some days.

I could remember when the wind had blown in my hair. When I smiled, and it was as if nothing was wrong in the world. It didn't matter that everything would eventually come crashing down around me, or that my soul would become tainted by the decisions I made—or those made *for* me by people who said they cared about me.

But I didn't need the breeze in my hair anymore. I didn't *need* the sun on my face. I only needed these walls. They were my safe space, the things protecting me.

I couldn't afford to risk anything else.

I sighed, once again pushing those thoughts away as I went back to work.

I had just closed my laptop and was stretching my back when the doorbell rang.

I froze, tension crawling up my spine and making my stomach turn sour. I tried not to let my pulse race, but I couldn't help it.

It couldn't be him. It couldn't be *them*.

It had to be someone else. Maybe it was the UPS driver.

Yes. That was it. It must be a delivery.

I looked down at my phone, bringing up the doorbell video app I had, and let out a sigh of relief.

It wasn't my past at my door.

It was Violet and the girls.

I could deal with them. They were good for me.

A visit from my friends wouldn't hurt.

At least, I hoped not.

I quickly ran my damp palms down the legs of my jeans before patting my cheeks, hoping they weren't too pale or too red. I needed to look normal.

Normal people didn't stress out or try to flee at the idea of someone being at their door.

They didn't want to vomit at the thought of not knowing who could be visiting.

I was fine. Everything would be fine.

My hands shook as I unlocked the deadbolt and then the second deadbolt, and then the handle lock itself.

When I opened the door, the girls each smiled at me. Sienna held cupcakes. Harmony had a bottle of sparkling juice. And Violet held out a charcuterie board.

I snorted, shaking my head.

"Ah, I see you've come prepared," I said, hoping my voice didn't sound as if I'd just had a minor heart attack.

They couldn't know. They couldn't find out who I had been in my past, the choices I'd made. I didn't want them to know why I screamed myself awake every night.

All they needed to know was that I was Meadow. I was normal. Safe.

As far as they were concerned, I didn't have a past—at least not one worth mentioning.

I took a step back, raising my brows as the girls walked in, chattering to one another even as they said hello.

"Well, we wanted to bring in a bit of a party before we forced you out of the house."

I closed the door behind me, doing my best to act nonchalant as I locked both deadbolts and the regular lock.

The girls didn't even notice. They had been here a couple of times before and were likely used to my antics. For all they knew, I was a single woman alone who wanted the extra security.

I pressed the keypad to make sure the security system was armed and then turned back to the others, a smile on my face. I hoped it reached my eyes.

"You guys didn't call or anything. A little weird. And shouldn't you be on your honeymoon now, Harmony?" I asked.

Harmony shook her head, tossing her gorgeous hair behind her shoulder. "Not for a bit. It's been three days since the wedding. I'm allowed to get out for some oxygen." Her cheeks turned red, and I shook my head, smiling as Sienna and Violet laughed.

"I'm surprised you can even walk," Sienna said. "I mean, with the way Brendon was all over you at the wedding? Yeah. Are you sure you haven't just escaped from being locked in the basement or something?"

I froze, the smile still on my face but no longer authentic. I was grateful that the others weren't looking at me.

I wasn't going to think about that night. Or *any* night from before. I was fine. Just fine.

"I'm allowed to leave. Brendon's at the bar with the guys, and I wanted to see my girls. So I showed up with cupcakes because I wanted to bake."

"And after Aiden stole one and said that they were '*okay, even though you aren't a chef,*' we brought them over," Sienna said, laughing.

"I am going to kick your man's ass one day," Harmony said. I sat back and watched as the others laughed and shared their inside jokes. They were dating or now married to brothers and were already a family in their own right. I was on the outside looking in, but that was where I wanted to be.

"Anyway, where have you been?" Violet asked.

I frowned. "Here? Where I am always."

"You say that, yet you haven't texted. No call. No note," Sienna said, perfecting her perfect British accent as she pretended that she was Molly Weasley from the *Harry Potter* series.

"I'm fine. Really. Just busy working. And after the wedding, I figured everyone would be busy with cleanup and honeymooning and everything that brides are supposed to do on their wedding night." I looked at Harmony, and she blushed even harder.

Apparently, she'd had a very nice wedding night.

"Well, considering you ran out of the reception, I wanted to make sure you were okay."

I looked at Violet, noting the concern in her eyes.

"I didn't run. I said goodbye."

"And then you ran like there was a demon on your tail," Sienna said. "We saw. Are you okay?"

"I didn't see," Harmony said quickly. "I was a little preoccupied. And I'm sorry about that. But what happened? Are you okay?"

We settled on the couches, and I set my hands in my lap.

I thought I'd hid things well. But from the way they looked at me now, I knew I hadn't been entirely successful.

I'd never been very good at hiding.

The bruises on my soul were evidence of that.

"It's fine."

"What's fine?" Violet asked, her voice stern.

"Beckham kissed me." I hadn't actually meant to say that. And as their eyes widened, and they leaned forward, I knew I was in for it.

Well…crap.

That secret was supposed to go with me to the grave. The kiss hadn't meant anything. It couldn't.

"He did? Did you not want it?" Sienna asked, frowning. "Because

I'll kick his ass for you, or I'll have Aiden do it if that's the case. He may be big and bearded and a little broody—although he's not really bearded right now since he shaved for the wedding—but anyway, I will totally kick his ass if I need to. Or have it kicked."

I shook my head quickly as Sienna continued to ramble.

"I'm fine. Really. He didn't hurt me. Didn't do anything wrong. But it can never happen again. It can't. Totally not going there again."

I slammed my mouth shut as the girls looked at me expectantly.

What was wrong with me? I was never like this. I was good at letting people know parts of myself, but they didn't need to know this part. And, honestly, I didn't want to relive it.

But as my friends waited, I knew I had to tell them something. But not everything.

"I was in a bad relationship once. I'm not ready to date yet."

I didn't know if I would ever be ready.

They nodded, and Violet reached out and gripped my hand. She gave it a squeeze, and I squeezed back, though not as long as I might have wanted to.

"Well, if you need anything, we're here for you. You don't have to keep it all bottled up."

"Bottling things up isn't good."

I looked at Sienna and then the other two, and I knew they were talking about their own experiences and thinking about Alison. I didn't want to worry them. Though I didn't know what to say.

So I simply smiled and took a cupcake.

"I'm really okay. I was a bit surprised that I kissed Beckham back. That's all. But we're going to be friends like always. Nothing more, nothing less. Don't worry about me. Now, tell me all about the rest of the reception that I missed. And I'm going to devour this cupcake. I'm just saying."

The way they looked at me told me that they didn't quite believe me, but that was fine.

I didn't really believe myself. As long as they didn't push, everything would be okay.

I didn't know what I would say if they *did* try to get more out of me.

We finished the plate of cupcakes, and all of the cheese and crackers and other goodness from the charcuterie board, and then I leaned back, my stomach full. I felt content.

It was still odd to have girlfriends. It wasn't something I'd had before this. It wasn't allowed.

But this was nice. I didn't feel quite so alone.

"Okay, well, we were going to take you to the bar to go meet our men, but we don't have to force you out if you don't want to go," Harmony said, helping me clean up.

I looked at the others as they tried to appear busy and held back a wince.

I didn't want people to feel as if they needed to be *careful* around me.

Worrying them wasn't something I wanted.

And I didn't want to be a liar. If everything were truly going to be okay, I knew I had to leave the house. At least, for a little bit.

"It'll be great. I'll join you, and everything will go back to normal. Just let me change, okay?" I asked.

"I don't even know if Beckham is working tonight," Violet said.

"Oh. That's good."

"Yeah, we can hang out and pester Dillon about what his plans are for the rest of his life," Harmony said, smiling. "Maybe you can get something out of him. He trusts you. And that's good."

I nodded and then went off to change while the others no doubt chatted about me in the living room.

I didn't mind. They could talk all they wanted. It wasn't as if they'd ever guess the person I once was. Uncover the fallout of the choices I'd made. And if I kept pretending that everything was normal and okay, maybe it actually would be.

Though I didn't know if it was good or not that Dillon trusted me.

I didn't know if anyone should.

Because there was always the threat of people coming. And once those looking for me found me, I didn't think anyone around me would be safe. Especially not the man who'd kissed me. The one who'd slid into my dreams every night since. No, not him. Especially him.

Chapter 3

Beckham

I was running late. And I never did that. I cursed my missed alarm. The fact that I actually needed one annoyed me even more. I'd set it and then had slept through the damn thing. It didn't matter that it had been bright outside after a late shift at the bar. I'd snored right through it.

I usually woke up before my alarm, even if I took a nap in the afternoon. I had long since trained my body to sleep in small bursts so I could get the rest I needed and still work when I had to.

It had been necessary when I was younger, while pulling the shit I did. There was no sleeping in my old life. There hadn't been time. I was always on the go, trying to stir up the next pot of crap. It hadn't mattered that I hurt people. Wasn't important that I took the easy way out or that I joined up at all.

I wasn't that person anymore. I couldn't be. But I still had some old habits that I had yet to break. Namely, being able to sleep no matter what time it was, thanks to my bartender's schedule.

However, even though I was usually pretty damn good at waking up on my own, I hadn't today.

Probably because I'd spent my entire sleep cycle tossing and turning and dreaming about a certain person I shouldn't be thinking about at all.

And I really shouldn't have fucking kissed her.

But I hadn't been able to hold myself back. And even though she'd returned the kiss, she ran.

I was such a fucking asshole for even thinking I could touch her.

To believe that I had any rights where she was concerned.

I shook my head and did my best to push her out of my thoughts. It would be best if we had even more space from each other. I'd left her alone the past couple of days. She'd run from me that night. And even though I'd felt a connection, she ran. So I wouldn't push. At least, not much.

Fuck. No. Not at all. I couldn't. Not given who she was. Or at least who she was *before*. Who *I* was in my past.

I walked into the bar, nodded at a couple of regulars, and tossed my stuff in my little cubby before lifting my chin at Brendon.

"Are you seriously behind the bar again?" I asked, the humor in my voice real. I loved needling Brendon. The guy was a good man. He was smart as hell and had more business savvy in his pinky than I had in my whole body. He was caring, funny, and apparently pretty good-looking, at least if you asked his new bride. But he wasn't the best part-time bartender. Oh, he was good, just not the best Connolly at it. And he damn sure wasn't as good as I was. Considering that Brendon loved being the best at everything and tried his hardest to do so, I had fun giving him shit.

Even though I knew it got under the man's skin. Hey, everybody needed a hobby.

"Fuck you. You're late," he grumbled as he poured two drafts and slid them over to waiting hands.

"I am. So you decided to take my place and ruin your bar?" I grinned and took the ticket for the next order.

"You're an asshole. I should fire you."

"No, I'm the best thing you have here."

"Excuse me, *I'm* the best thing we have here." Aiden puffed out his chest as he came around the corner with two plates in his hands. It looked as if they held some form of tapas, an appetizer thing that usually didn't fit well in the bar scene. But the Connollys had spruced up the place and changed the food a bit, thanks to Aiden and his gift. Aiden Connolly had worked at a Michelin-starred restaurant. He could be a famous chef anywhere in the world. But, instead, he had come back to his family and seemed to be setting down some roots. Maybe the guy would open up a restaurant of his own someday. Perhaps even with his little brother Dillon, if the kid decided to take that path.

But until that happened, I knew I would get some really damn good food from the man, and I was thankful that he had decided to *slum* it in the bar scene.

"Oh, shut up," Brendon grumbled.

"Wow, you sure are acting a bit growly and unsatisfied for a man who recently got married." Aiden met my gaze over Brendon's back as the other man bent down to pick something up from the floor. I winked and continued down our current line of conversation. "Yeah. You having a tough time there? Things not up to the standards you're used to?"

"Yeah, things hanging low?" Aiden asked.

"I'm going to kill you both. And, for your information, my wife is over in that corner. And she could probably kick both of your asses. You're lucky I don't do it myself."

The hair on the back of my neck stood on end, and I looked over to the corner because I knew—just *knew*—that if Harmony was there, she wasn't alone. And, yeah, I was right.

Violet and Sienna were on one side of the booth, laughing with each other as Harmony said something.

And right next to Harmony, in the position closest to me, where she would face me if she turned her head even a fraction of an inch, was Meadow.

Fucking hell.

I should have known that she would be here. The night I was late because I had been too busy trying not to jerk off to dreams about her. After I'd decided that we should stay friends and that I needed to keep away from her in other ways. Thinking maybe we shouldn't even be *that* close.

Of course she was here.

She liked it here. At least, I thought she did.

This was her place. Her friends were all over the damn bar. Some of them were my bosses.

Now I had to figure out what the fuck to do about it.

"If your wife's over there, then why are you behind the bar?" Aiden asked, smiling at one of the customers at the counter. Aiden didn't smile at anyone much, so he must be in a good mood.

He'd probably gotten laid by his girl before he came to work. *Must be nice.*

I'd lost count of the number of months it had been since I'd gotten laid. Probably since before I saw Meadow again for the first time.

No, that couldn't be right. I'd gone out with that girl, Julie, a few months ago. Right?

Dear God. It had been a few months. No wonder I was hard up and having dreams about girls I shouldn't be fantasizing about. I was just horny. Soon as I found someone at the bar, I'd take them home and fix that. I'd make sure the girl had the best night of her life, and then I'd be fine for a while. Just top one off.

God, I was such a fucking lecher in my head.

"This asshole was late"—he pointed at me—"so I had to help. It's nice that we're busy, though, right?" he asked, and I winced.

"Sorry, Brendon. You go sit with your wife. I'll get to work. I won't be late again."

Brendon's eyes widened a bit, and he met Aiden's gaze before looking at me. "Hey, I was only messing with you. You were like ten minutes late. You're usually thirty minutes early all the time. Don't worry about it. Are you okay?"

I nodded, giving him the smile I knew everyone expected of me. It was what I was good at. Being what people needed me to be.

"I'm good. Go sit with your woman. I've got this."

Brendon raised a brow. "I'm not that bad of a bartender. I know you like to make fun of me, but I'm not *that* bad."

Aiden snorted, pulling a draft before handing it over to a customer. "You're not the best."

"And you shouldn't be back here either," I said to Aiden, laughing. "Go cook. Brendon, go work your magic on the wife. I'm going to get to work. I've got this. Trust me with your baby. I know what I'm doing."

Brendon smiled. "Yeah. I guess you do. And we do trust you, you know, Beckham? We wouldn't have let you stay here for as long as you have, especially with your attitude, if we didn't."

He lifted his chin, smiled, and then went off towards the booth where the girls were seated.

I stood there in stunned silence for a moment, trying to collect my thoughts.

I couldn't remember the last time anyone had said they trusted me. Could they really at all? Sure, I tried to do the right thing, but it wasn't the same. Wasn't actual trustworthiness. And though I planned to do the best I could for the rest of my life to make sure I earned what they gave me, I wasn't positive I'd ever be worthy of it. Not with the sins that covered my body, the scars that would never go away, and the regret that ran through my veins.

"Hey, do you have that new IPA on tap?" a guy asked, and I turned around, giving him my best what-the-fuck look. Not that I didn't like IPAs. I enjoyed all beer. Some more than others. But I loved making the young guy squirm. He looked barely over twenty-one, but I remembered him. He had a real ID. I was pretty good at spotting the fake ones. And I knew the kid was probably twenty-two now. He could drink legally. But it was good to remind them of their place. And this one tipped better for it. He seemed to like being intimidated a bit. I didn't know why. But he did. So I indulged, and that meant more money for me. More cash for rent. More for food. And more to stockpile in case I had to go away. They would find me eventually. They always did. And *when* they did, I'd have to run. And…fuck. I didn't want to. I liked it here. Enjoyed the friends and the makeshift family I had made. I didn't want to leave. But I'd have to if they showed.

I looked up and met Meadow's gaze. I swallowed hard. Yes, I'd have to go. If they came, they would find her, too. And I didn't think she wanted to be found. I wouldn't be the person who ruined her peace.

I got to work, pulling beers and mixing drinks. There was a rush on martinis with twists tonight, and I had to wonder if someone had mentioned it. It wasn't on sale. But I was damn sure making them extra cold. It made me crave one, even though I didn't really like vodka. Or gin. I was a whiskey man.

"Hey, you going to take your break soon?" Cameron asked as he walked towards me. "Dillon's going to try to stop by a bit later. He's out with his friends tonight, the ones he's moving in with."

"Oh, yeah? How's that going?"

Cameron ran a hand over his face. "I don't fucking know. It's like watching my baby leave the house. And he's not even my kid."

"Stop lying to yourself. He's yours. You raised him. Maybe not from birth, but you raised him. And he's growing up, going to college, making friends. And now he's moving out on his own. He's doing damn well."

"You say that, but I'm afraid everything's going to get fucked up because I didn't do a good enough job."

I raised a brow and looked at the other man even as I pulled another draft. "That kid got into a private college, even after getting into the state one he's currently at. He's transferring this fall on a partial scholarship to a place that doesn't give a lot of them. He worked his ass off."

"He did. It'll be weird not having him at the school right downtown. Where he can simply walk over and see us during the day if we're here and he wants to."

"He'll still be close, though, right?"

"Yeah. It's just weird that he's growing up."

"He's nineteen, man. He's already grown up."

"Don't remind me."

"So you and Violet ever going to have kids of your own?" I asked, not even sure where that question had come from.

Cameron raised his brows. "Have to ask her to marry me first."

"You better get on that. I mean, Brendon's already hitched. And I think Sienna and Aiden are well on their way. You don't want Aiden to beat you, do you?"

"You're a shit-stirrer. And of course I don't want Aiden to beat me." He mumbled the last part, probably because he didn't want his woman to hear. As much as she loved the brothers, I didn't really think that Violet wanted to know that a proposal might be coming sooner rather than later only so Cameron could do it before Aiden did. Not that she'd say no. At least, I didn't *think* she would. All three couples were happy and in pre—and post—wedded bliss.

It was nice to see, even though I wanted no part of it for myself.

My gaze strayed to Meadow once again. She smiled at me, though it didn't quite reach her eyes.

Oh, good. Fuck this.

I was losing my damn mind. I really needed to get her out of my head.

But I didn't think I would be able to. After all, I hadn't been able to before, even when she was so off-limits that it probably would've meant someone literally slicing my throat if I moved in too close.

Those barriers weren't there as much anymore, but the remnants still remained. The shadows. I didn't want any part of that. Or, at least, I shouldn't.

"So, you're going to take your break?"

I shook my head. "Maybe another half hour. We're about to hit that lull, and I'll let Ben take over for a while. Sound good?"

Cameron nodded, took the beers I had poured for him, and headed over to the table.

Brendon and Cameron had already sat down, Aiden moving back

and forth between the booth and the kitchen. A big group had just finished getting their food, so I figured Aiden would wrap up for the night. He'd technically been off shift for the past hour, but the man never let his kitchen go without him for too long. He might trust his staff, but he was very anal-retentive when it came to his food. I didn't mind, though. It was damn good grub.

Thirty minutes passed, and the lull indeed came. I nodded at Ben, who took control of the bar, and I went back to the storeroom. I'd make sure that we had everything ready for when I got back, and then I would actually take my break.

As soon as I turned the corner and passed the billiards area where we'd hosted a pool tournament at one point, Meadow walked from the other direction. She'd probably come from the bathroom area.

I wanted to touch her. Wanted to be close to her.

She did something to me that made no sense. But I was stronger than these feelings. I had to be. When she looked up, and her eyes widened, I knew I wasn't resilient enough to resist her.

I was a fucking bastard, and I didn't care anymore. I'd tried to be good for so long. Had even succeeded in some respects, but I wasn't going to be good anymore. I didn't think I could be.

"Oh. I didn't know you were back here," she said, her voice a little breathy.

I leaned against the wall, blocking her way. Then I smirked. I knew she hated that. Every time I did it, her eyes narrowed, and a little crease formed on her brow.

But her eyes always went to my mouth, so maybe she didn't hate it *that* much.

"Just coming back here before I take my break. Why don't you take it with me?" Jesus Christ, that was the worst line ever. I wasn't very good at things like that, especially when it came to her. But that was fine. I wasn't good at many things.

"I think we're okay. We had enough of that already, didn't we?"

Surprised that she had alluded to the kiss, I raised a single brow.

"You *did* kiss me back."

"And then I ran away." Her voice was a little sharp, and I blinked.

"I figured you had to be home by midnight or something."

"I'm not Cinderella. I didn't go home in a pumpkin. I took a Lyft." She raised a brow in response. "Honestly, I'm surprised your ego can fit in this hallway. Just saying."

"Well, it's a heavy burden to bear, but I manage. You should go out with me."

Fuck, why did I say that?

"No. Never." Her voice shook a bit, and she lowered her gaze. "I can't."

Jesus Christ. I knew she couldn't. Why we shouldn't. I didn't think she knew all of it, though. "Meadow." I reached out and lifted her chin as I gently caressed her skin. "You don't have to be wary of me."

Or should she be?

"I'm not afraid of you." I didn't know if I could taste the lie, but it definitely didn't sound entirely truthful.

"We could be friends, though. Right?"

"That kiss wasn't about friendship."

"No, it wasn't. But we have a lot of mutual friends. You're going to be coming into this bar often with them. That means you'll have to deal with me. Maybe we should make sure that we stay friends."

"Only friends?"

"Jesus. I don't know. I like you. I want you. And you want me. I can tell. Let's do something about it." I paused. "If you only want to be friends? Then I'll do my best to keep things that way."

She snorted and shook her head. But she didn't pull back. My fingers were still on her skin. Still gently caressing. Damn it, she was such a temptation. I needed to step away.

"Like I said. Ego much?"

"I like my big...ego." I didn't look down at my crotch when I said it, but she did.

A pretty blush stained her cheeks, and I grinned.

"Come out with me."

"I shouldn't. I can't."

"Shouldn't and can't are two very different things. Which one is it, baby?"

And then I lowered my head and fell into the abyss and my bad decisions. I kissed her again, a brush of lips, a sweet caress of sin.

My tongue snaked out, parting her lips, and she moaned. But she didn't pull away. Instead, she put her hands on my chest, her fingernails digging into my flesh through my shirt.

And when I stepped back, her pupils were large, dark. Her throat worked as she swallowed hard.

"I shouldn't."

"Maybe not. But let's try it out anyway."

I really should not be doing this. Just like she shouldn't. There was only one way this ended. Actually, there were two possibilities. Heartache or death. Or both.

But I didn't care. So when she nodded, just a little movement, a way to say yes, something twisted inside me.

I didn't want to hurt her, but I craved her. But I craved her.

I only hoped that with that "*yes*," that one little nod, I hadn't sealed our fates.

It had happened once already. *At least* once. For both of us.

I didn't know if we could survive it again.

Chapter 4

I'm not perfectly imperfect. Just imperfect.
~Meadow, journal entry

Meadow

Women got asked out all the time. Men, too. Everybody did.

I was no different than anyone else. I'd succumbed and nodded yes to Beckham.

And that meant that tomorrow, on his day off, we were going on a date. I didn't know what kind. It wasn't like I had much experience with them. I sucked at the whole dating thing, actually. My *dating* usually included putting on tight jeans, high-heeled boots, a bra that pushed my boobs up to my chin, and then involved me sitting on the back of a bike before doing things I shouldn't.

At least, old Meadow's dates had been like that.

The new Meadow didn't do that. She didn't go out at all.

I hadn't been on a date since Coby.

I shuddered at the name, wondering why I'd even thought it. I'd done my best *not* to think about him for over a year. It wouldn't do to start now. Simply because I thought of my past for some reason every time I thought of Beckham didn't mean that was the right trajectory.

Sure, he was big and bearded and tattooed like Coby, but that didn't mean he was the same type of man Coby was.

Though it surprised me a little that I'd said yes to Beckham, or that I wanted to kiss or be near him at all. Even the similarities in the way the two of them moved worried me—or at least it *should.*

I knew that I flinched when large men came near. I knew I cowered even though I tried not to.

I hadn't always been like this. I used to laugh and smile and toss my hair behind my shoulders, grinning at any man who flirted with me. But I didn't flirt back. Not usually. And especially not when Coby and I were together. He didn't like that. And I hadn't *wanted* to flirt with anyone else while I was with him. He was mine. My prize, my dream, my…everything. He had been the epitome of everything a girl needed.

He had a rough edge, and paired with his wicked smile and growl, he was the ultimate bad boy. I'd thought he was nice, even under the cruelty. In his position, he'd needed to be that way. You couldn't work your way up in the club without being a little ruthless. You had to push and fight your way to the top, and he'd had to do that more than most. His father was the president of the MC. Still was as far as I knew. And just because Coby was the son, the legacy, didn't mean he could rise easily.

Coby had done things I didn't want to think about, even now. And he'd started them before we even met.

But that had been my life, too.

I'd grown up with that.

Not in the same club, but another one.

Both had been the type to skirt the edges of the law, and they usually came out on the wrong side.

I looked down at my hands, at the tiny scars on my wrists and my fingertips.

I'd fallen off a bike—or, more accurately, I had been pushed off. But I'd survived.

Back then, I was an old lady. Coby's property. His bitch. He called me his one and only.

And I had treasured it. I'd watched my mother climb through the ranks along with my father until he became the president of their MC. And I was the princess. The one who finally fell in love with the prince of another club. Thankfully, they weren't rivals, and I hadn't gone all Juliet and Romeo, but there was plenty of drama and angst regardless. And, at first, I was only a teenager. Then I became an adult who made her own choices—ones that I regretted to this day.

But I wasn't that person anymore. I was normal. I *had* to be.

I was just Meadow. The one who went to school and got her

degrees. The one who wrote and edited science textbooks. I rarely left the house, and if I did, it wasn't to go anyplace where anyone from my past might be.

I wasn't that person anymore.

But I had said "yes" to Beckham.

Not that he was my past. He had nothing to do with that life. He was only a bartender. A friend of a friend, who could be *my* friend in truth.

Maybe I agreed because old Meadow was coming out. But not the kindhearted one with the soft eyes. The one who'd fought and clawed her way to the top alongside Coby because that had been the only thing I *could* do.

I hadn't been cruel like the rest of them. I hadn't been mean or hard-hearted.

But I hadn't thought myself anything more than what I was, either. I hadn't considered myself worthy.

When Coby hit me for the first time, I didn't fight back. My father had beaten my mother enough, had told her that if she didn't toe the line, if she ruined his chances of moving up, that she would regret it.

So, while I knew that my mom didn't deserve to be hit—like the punch to the face I got wasn't warranted—I also knew that, sometimes, you couldn't get around it.

Often, if you didn't find a way out, it was your destiny.

So I hadn't walked away the first time Coby hit me. Hadn't left the second, either.

I stayed because I had nothing else.

There was no way I could go back to my parents, not when they'd sent me off in grand style as their princess to marry the future king.

I broke a little inside, shattered into a thousand pieces with each blow, every time Coby looked at me like I was nothing.

But I hadn't left. Hadn't run away.

There was nowhere to go.

It was only when he got drunk enough to bring a friend into our bed to see what I would do that I tried to fight back.

He didn't force me, neither of them had, but they didn't leave me standing in the end, either.

No, they left me bleeding, a broken shell of myself. I tried to crawl away, attempted to run.

I still had the scar on my back from the knife—a cut to prove that I was his. That there would be no leaving him…ever.

So I stayed.

Because I had to. There was nothing left for me out there. Nothing left of me within either.

When my parents heard about what I had done, that I'd tried to leave, my dad took me in hand to make sure that I never attempted to run away again. The scar on my left knee was proof of that.

I made a move to run one more time, but they didn't let me.

I had scars on both ankles from that incident.

Rope burns from when they tied me up so I'd learn whose property I was.

It wasn't until I ran with evidence of their drug-running that I felt even remotely safe.

I snitched. I became the worst sort of person in my family's eyes, in Coby's eyes. But I needed that freedom.

I'd caught a glimpse of the person I was becoming, of the woman that I could turn into, and I saw my mother.

I didn't want to become that. I wanted more. So I got out. Finally.

Coby was in jail now. He could never hurt me again.

They hadn't sent him to jail for hurting me, or for threatening me.

No, he had gone down for drugs. They were worth more than a woman's body in Coby's world. More than her soul.

After all, I had basically sold myself to them. What, of what was left, was worth anything?

I tried not to be bitter about that, but sometimes, that vitriol was all I had.

But none of that mattered now. I was out of that life. Completely out of it.

I tried not to talk to my parents. They came to me for money, but I'd tried to leave that life fully after Coby had been locked up.

The state didn't even require me to testify since my help had gotten them all the evidence they needed.

Coby had pleaded for less time, so I didn't even have to face him in court. Didn't have to face any of the club's members.

Yet I knew my life was still on the line if I wasn't careful.

"Stop it, Meadow," I mumbled to myself, shaking my head.

I went to the fridge and poured myself a glass of wine, chugging it in three big gulps before pouring myself another.

I needed to take the edge off, to be okay for a brief moment. I didn't know why thinking about going on a date with Beckham had made me think of all of that from my past. Maybe because I hadn't actually been on a date before, at least not with Coby.

I wasn't normal. And I wasn't good at pretending. I didn't know if I had ever been good at it.

My phone buzzed, bringing me out of my thoughts, and I froze as I looked down at the name on the readout.

I didn't want to answer.

"Just get it over with," I whispered to myself. As soon as the screen went black, and I knew she had hung up, it lit up again, this time with a new call. My mother would keep calling until I answered. She didn't understand that I needed time or space.

I picked up this time, steadying myself as I sucked in a deep breath. "Hello."

"You don't answer your phone?"

Petal Brown's voice grated on my ears, but I was used to it. It sounded as if she had smoked a pack a day, which she most likely had, but she also made sure that it was a little low, a bit breathy for my dad. I hated that I knew that, but it was kind of hard to put that away and forget about it, especially when it was something he said to her often. He hadn't cared that I was around. He was horrible.

My mom hadn't been a terrible mother all the time. And that was something I needed to remind myself of.

I remembered the days when we played outside and laughed. Or when she'd dance with me in the rain or giggle and sneak me an ice cream cone without my dad knowing. I remembered how the sun shone on her bottle-blond hair, and I could recall thinking, *you're the most beautiful woman in the world.*

At least, on the outside.

I hadn't cared that she bleached her hair, or that she was always afraid of her roots going gray or dark.

I dyed my hair a darker brown now because I liked the color, and I wanted to be a new Meadow instead of the one with the ash-blond hair with natural highlights that Coby loved.

Or, at least, pretended to.

As my mother began to berate me over the phone about not answering and how I was a disgrace and an ingrate, I tried to ignore it.

I attempted to remember the good times. But there hadn't been many.

She'd slapped me when I said too many things I shouldn't, or when I questioned my father or the club. She'd pinched me behind the arms where the bruises wouldn't show if I didn't say the right things. She forced me to shove my fingers down my throat if I overate at dinner. And she'd smack me on the behind if I didn't do the right things for Daddy like having the table set for dinner or wearing the right clothes that he would approve of.

She'd wanted me skinny and perfect with the best boobs that could fill a push-up bra. When I was fifteen, she'd told me she had been trying to scrimp for money to get me a boob job like she had, all because I hadn't filled out the way she wanted. But then hormones and genes had done their best, and she'd scrapped the idea, using the money to buy herself things instead.

I hadn't wanted a boob job. I'd liked my body, even as a teenager. But what I thought or felt hadn't mattered to Mom.

She put me in too-tight jeans, leather skirts, bustiers, and other barely-there outfits to try and entice the other MC's members. I had to be the perfect princess in a world that was anything *but* perfect.

Then, when I met Coby, and he treated me far differently than anyone else had, my mother thought I'd done the best thing in the world. She believed that I had become the woman she thought I should have been all along.

But I hadn't. I wasn't that person. Or maybe I *had* become what she wanted, and it wasn't enough.

Either way, the woman on the other end of the phone call now had given birth to me. Raised me.

And yet, she'd never loved me.

I didn't think she could.

"Are you even fucking listening to me?" she asked, and I brought myself out of my thoughts.

"I'm sorry. What is it you wanted?"

"Answer your fucking door." She hung up the phone, and then the doorbell rang over and over and over again.

I froze, sweat sliding down my back as my palms went clammy.

My mother had never shown up at my house before. She shouldn't be here, but it appeared she was.

I hadn't changed my name or gone into true hiding, so it wasn't like she *couldn't* find me. After Coby had gone to jail, and my parents told me that they disowned me, no one really cared where I ended up. I told myself I was hiding, but in reality, I was just trying to be a different person and start over somewhere else.

And yet, here we were.

She was here.

The doorbell rang again. I could hear her screaming on the other side.

"I will wake up your whole fucking neighborhood, young lady. Open this fucking door right now."

I closed my eyes, counted to ten. I didn't want to believe this was happening. That she was right outside my door. I didn't want to wake up the whole neighborhood. I didn't want this to be happening, but it wasn't like I could stop it or simply will it away.

My past was here. I couldn't hide from it anymore.

I went to the door, tugging my sweatshirt over my hips. I looked like hell, but I didn't care. Yet, I did. What would she say when she looked at me?

Would it matter?

I didn't know, but I would find out soon.

I opened the door, flipping each lock carefully as I did.

I could have called the cops, alerted my security, but I didn't. This was my mother. And even though she was yelling and cursing at me, I somehow still hoped that things would be different.

Or maybe I knew that if I didn't get this over with now, she would keep coming back.

"It's about fucking time." She stormed past me, pushing my shoulder as she did. "Looks like you've done well for yourself. Not my taste, but it's fine." She looked me up and down, staring. "Good God. You're never going to keep Coby if you dress like that. What the hell are you wearing? Jesus, that sweatshirt's hiding...what? The extra twenty pounds you've added? You're such a fat-ass. You always were. If I hadn't kept on you when you were little, you never would have gotten Coby. And all your weight had to go to your hips and your thighs. Never to your tits. You know, that comes from my mother-in-law. Daddy's mama. She is such a lard-ass. Constantly having to wear sweats and leggings and stuff because she can't fit into her leathers anymore. God. If you don't take care of yourself, Coby's never going to take you back. You better work on that. I only say this because I love you. Us girls need to watch our weight. You can't let yourself be too big. Fat kills. It keeps men away."

I just stood there, looking at her, wondering how in the hell this woman had raised me. Every single thing she said was wrong. I liked the way I looked. I was nowhere close to being what some might call overweight. And even if I *was* what some might classify as that, what the fuck ever?

As long as I was happy and took care of myself, fuck them. I had curves, and I liked them.

Jesus Christ.

"Why are you here?" I asked, surprised my voice was still steady.

"I'm here so you can do your duty."

I folded my arms over my chest. "What do you mean?"

"Your daddy and I need a little help. It's been a tough couple of months since I asked for anything…with what happened after you left. You know, *the incident.*"

I looked at her, not quite comprehending. I left when the cops raided both places looking for drugs. They'd found all of them, but only a few people had gone to jail. Coby being one of them. My father hadn't. Neither had Mom.

"You need money," I said, comprehending at last.

"Just a little. You know you owe us. *For everything.* We gave everything we ever had to get you where you are. You owe us for that, at least."

"I went to school on my own. I took out loans and attended community college. I worked night and day to get myself through. *I* did this."

"And you would have none of this if we hadn't put clothes on your back and food in your belly as a kid. Don't be such an ungrateful bitch."

It didn't surprise me that she kept calling me horrible names and degrading me even as she asked for things. That's how Petal Brown was. There was no changing that.

Mom had been named after a flower her mother saw on her way to the hospital. Somehow, my mother had come out alive and healthy as a baby, at least according to my grandparents, even though Grandma had been high as fuck when she gave birth. Hence the name.

Petal had wanted to continue the tradition with names since you could find flowers in meadows. At least, that's what she said. Dad told me it was because of where I was conceived, though he hadn't used those words. No, he'd used ones far more crass.

Somewhere deep down, I truly hated my family. Or at least what they had become. I didn't want to be a part of this. I wanted to be alone. In my own home.

The place this woman was currently tainting. I knew if I didn't give her some money now, she wouldn't leave.

Even if I told myself that I shouldn't give her anything and hope that she never came back again, that wasn't how things worked with her. She would stay, and she would make a scene, and she would find me at the bar or with my friends or somewhere else later, and it would be worse.

I didn't want things to be worse.

So I went to my wallet, pulled out the couple of twenties I had, and handed them over. "It's all I have. I'm sorry."

"This is it?" she asked, sneering. "Well, I guess you're not as high and mighty as you think." Still, she stuffed the money into her bra without saying, "*thank you*."

"Call your pops. He misses you."

He didn't. He missed the idea of having the perfect princess to lord over the guys. He didn't miss me.

"And visit Coby. He needs you."

"No, he really doesn't," I whispered. I hadn't meant to say anything. "You should leave now. You have your money. It's all I have. You need to go."

"You were always such an ungrateful brat. Even when I made sure that you were perfect for Coby. As I said, he's going to need you. I'll leave. Sure, honey, I'll go. But remember this. Once you're in, you're never out."

"I didn't really have much choice, did I?"

"Well, you had a choice when you said yes to Coby. When you spread your legs for him and became his whore. There's no getting out after that. There's no saying no. But don't worry. You'll see when he gets out. His appeal is coming up soon. You'll have to deal with him then."

The threat slid over me. My hands went damp, and my blood turned cold.

"Go. Go away."

My voice was firm, even though I wanted to scream.

"Okay. Thanks for the money. You're going to do your mama proud." She reached up and pinched my cheek before slapping it a couple of times, two quick, hard taps like she was patting me. It wasn't only that.

Then she left, sauntering out in her tight jeans and frizzy hair.

I closed the door behind her, flipping all three locks afterwards, and then slid to the floor, my hands shaking.

I wasn't part of that world anymore. I couldn't be. This wasn't some movie where a biker gang came in and took me away. This was real life. I had made choices, and I was going to continue making them. Even though my mother would likely always say things like she just did. I knew Coby wasn't getting out anytime soon. And he certainly didn't need me.

My mother might know where I lived, but no one else in the clubs did. No one cared.

I was only their forgotten whore. At least, that's what they called me when they asked for money. And that was okay, that's all I needed to be with them.

I needed to be Meadow. My own person.

As the tears slid down my cheeks, and bile rose in my throat, I wondered how I was going to be that person.

How could I be normal for Beckham and go out on a date and pretend that everything was fine? Nothing was fine.

And it wasn't going to be.

I looked down at my hands and then wiped my face, trying to catch my breath. No, it *had* to be okay. I needed it to be all right. I would make sure of it.

I was going on that date, and I would be normal.

I needed that.

I wouldn't let them win. If I backed away, if I hid again, if I cried myself into oblivion, they would win.

I didn't think I had it in me to let that happen.

Chapter 5

Beckham

Sometimes, you had to break down and ask for the wisdom of those who knew more than you did. In my case, it was the knowledge of a nineteen-year-old.

"Dillon. I need your help."

The kid looked up, a sly smile on his face as a lock of hair flopped down over his eyes.

Sometimes, he reminded me of Shawn Mendes with the way his hair curled a little bit if he let it grow, and how he always had a smile for others. I knew that Dillon hadn't had the easiest life growing up, even though Cameron had tried to make it easier for him. But the Connolly brothers—at least those who were genetically related—hadn't had the best birth mother.

Their foster mom had been fucking fantastic. I'd only met her a few times before she passed away, but I liked Rose. However, she wasn't here to help me. And I knew from past experience that if she were here, I would likely be asking her for advice. However, I'd have to take what I could get. And Dillon, the sage and wise one when it came to romance, was the person I needed.

"Let me see, does it have anything to do with Meadow?" he asked, and I narrowed my eyes. "How did you know that?"

"Because everybody asks me about women these days. I don't get asked much about anything else. Although I don't really know when I became the love guru."

"You're anything but that, kid."

"You say that, and yet, here you are. Asking me about Meadow. So what can I do for you?"

"You sound a bit cocky. Maybe I shouldn't ask for your help."

Dillon shrugged, though there was sincerity in his eyes. Maybe he wasn't so cocky.

"I read romance, and therefore, I happen to understand a little more about women than my brothers. Or at least more than they thought I knew. Not that I know a lot. But I can help you talk it out. What do you need?"

"You're saying that you read romance books, and that's how you could figure out how to help each of your brothers with the issues they had with their women?"

I'd never read a romance novel. Not that I hated them or anything, but I didn't really have time to read. In my old life, nobody read. If you did, you got your ass kicked. And now, I was a little too busy, and it just wasn't my hobby. Maybe I needed to make it one. If I did, a romance book would be the first thing I picked up.

"It's not a be-all, end-all, but they're written by women for women, at least according to their taglines or whatever. So, yeah, I learned a few things. Plus, now that I have a sister-in-law and a bunch of future sisters-in-law, I tend to figure things out by watching. Maybe."

I narrowed my eyes. "Maybe?"

"I don't know. You guys keep coming to me. I didn't actually seek this position out. Like, what if when I actually find someone I really like, I suck at this, and no one's there to help *me*?"

I looked at him then, shaking my head. "You have your entire family. And you have me. I might not be blood, but when and if you actually need to talk to me about women or whatever you're having an issue with, I'll be here for you. Okay? You won't be alone."

"Thanks. Although, if you're coming to me for help, maybe I don't *want* to go to you for help." He smiled as he said it, and I wanted to punch the kid—good-naturedly, of course.

"You're an asshole. But I kind of like you. However, I really do need your help. For real. And yes, it's about Meadow."

"Okay. Ask away."

"I have no idea where to take her on our date."

I didn't mention that this would be my first date. The first of my life. And not only with Meadow. Sure, I had taken women out before, but it was different back then. You didn't really *date* women. They sort of…fell into your life. Jesus Christ, I hated my old ways. I was such an asshole. I didn't remember the women I'd been with, and I sure as hell did not remember their names.

That was something I'd changed after I left. I knew every woman I'd been with since—not that there had been many. I didn't want to treat women like that. I wasn't a horrible person. Everything had been consensual. And I made sure they got off like I did. But I never respected them the way I should have. I saw that now. Once I was out of that life, I vowed to change. And now, I was going to make sure that Meadow knew I was all about her. Only I didn't know how to go about doing that.

"You have no idea where you want to take Meadow, then?"

"No clue."

"Well, that's not too uncommon. Dates are expensive these days. And you don't know if you want to spend time talking, so you want to go to a place that's not too loud and where you can actually hear each other. Or if you want to spend some quiet time alone, a movie will do that. Though if you do dinner and a movie, that adds up timewise, and I don't know if you actually have that much time for a date. So, what do you want out of this date?"

I wanted for Meadow to be happy. And for me not to make a mistake. But I didn't say that aloud. That probably wouldn't help the situation. I already knew I would most likely make some mistakes while doing this.

"I want to give her a good time. Something that will make her feel like she's the center of my universe. At least for the evening."

Dillon grinned, his smile so wide, I knew that if any woman could see him, they would probably swoon. The kid was good-looking, and one day when he finally figured out what he wanted—and not only in life, but also with sharing his life—the women were going to come in droves. And some were probably bound for heartache. Like with any good Connolly brother.

"I think anything you do with her will make her feel like that. I see the way you look at her."

I winced. "Yeah, I don't know if that's the best thing for you to be seeing, kid."

"You don't look at her like you're some deranged psycho or anything."

"Well, that's good," I said with a laugh.

"Yes. So, what does she really know about you? What do you think she'll like that you do?"

"She sees me at the bar. Knows that I'm friends with her friends. That's about it."

"Okay. So maybe don't take her to a bar. She already knows that about you. Show her something different."

"Like what? I'm pretty much only the bar these days."

Not that I minded that. It was better than my life only being about my bike. Or the friends I had. The ones that hadn't been true friends at all.

"Seriously, I have no idea, kid. I figured going out to dinner would be fine. She can order whatever she wants and have a glass of wine, and then I'll take her home." I closed my eyes, pinching the bridge of my nose. "Dear God. I have no idea what I'm doing."

"That's not that bad. I mean, it's just a normal date, right?"

I didn't know what a *normal date* was. But, again, I didn't tell the kid that. No one needed to know that I hadn't actually been on a real date before. What I'd done before was certainly not *dating*. Meadow was unique. Special. And that scared me.

"I don't know," I ground out.

"Okay, dinner, wine, and talking is the perfect date. You can make it casual or fancy or whatever you want. It's Meadow. She's sweet, and she smiles, even though she doesn't talk a lot. But she's always there for those who need her, no matter what they need. I mean, she helped Violet through her migraines, still does whenever Cameron can't be there. She likes helping others. And I know she likes music," Dillon added. My eyes widened.

"You're right. She always dances in her seat when no one's looking whenever there's a good song on. When we had that live band in, she hummed along."

"See? You do know her."

I frowned, thumbing my fingers along the aged wood of the table. There were still people in the bar, some eating their lunches and talking. There weren't too many drinkers yet, and that was good, considering it was still a little early, and I wasn't working behind the bar. I didn't have a shift at all today, but I had come in to chat with Dillon. He was on the schedule as a bar-back, so I knew I could catch him.

The fact that his brothers might be around any minute to harass me was something I might have to deal with. But I would.

"There's something I can do. Something she might like. Or it could be a completely stupid idea."

The plan started to form in my mind, and I really hoped she liked it. And I really, really hoped I wouldn't make a fool of myself. However, I was quite good at that, so…who knew? Maybe it helped.

"Are you going to tell me what it is?" Dillon asked, and I shook my head.

"No, but you helped. I will think on it a bit more. And, hopefully, she'll like it."

"Well, now that the suspense is eating at me, I hope you do it so you can tell me about it after."

I looked at him and grinned. "If she likes it, I promise I'll tell you."

"And if she doesn't like it, we're going to forget it ever happened?" Dillon asked, grinning.

"Yeah, that sounds about right. Thanks for this, kid."

"No problem. Just remember your promise. When I fuck up with a girl and have no idea what I'm doing, be there. Okay?"

I narrowed my eyes at him and gave him a tight nod. "If I'm around, I promise I'll be there."

Dillon opened his mouth, presumably to ask what that meant, but I quickly shook my head and got up, waving goodbye. I hadn't meant to say that first part, but it was the truth. I didn't know how long I'd be around. I'd been here for a while. And I was afraid that if I stayed any longer, things might end up bad for Meadow.

So, of course, I was doing the stupidest thing ever. I was taking her out.

I really hoped she liked what I had planned.

"A piano bar?" Meadow asked from my side, and I slid my hand around hers, giving it a squeeze. Her eyes widened slightly, her mouth parting with a sharp intake of breath at my touch. I slid my thumb over her knuckles, her soft skin so tempting beneath mine.

I had gone to her house to pick her up like I'd promised, though I hadn't gone inside. I noticed the double deadbolts and the fact that she seemed to be using them even during the day. I was happy about that. Considering what I knew of her past, it was a damn good idea.

Not that I wanted to think about that or how she could be in danger.

She was safe. She had to be. If she weren't, something would have likely happened well before now.

But the fact that she was taking care of herself? Yeah, that was a damn good thing.

When she opened the door, though, I'd lost all thought, and had to take a minute to actually remember to breathe.

She looked so damn sexy.

My gaze moved over her now, and I couldn't help but grin.

She wore tight, black leather leggings, and I only knew that they were leggings because Violet had a similar pair and had been talking about them at the bar with the girls.

I swore, sometimes, they forgot that I was one of the guys and didn't need to hear about all of that. But I didn't mind. That just meant I knew that Meadow was wearing a pair now, and I could appreciate them. She had on a top that went to her neck, so she wasn't showing cleavage, but her shirt sort of piled on itself with fabric and looked like she had roses and flowers all over her chest.

She had on a linen jacket or some other type of fabric that I couldn't name, and she looked sexy as hell in black and wine-red.

Even with the leather, she still dressed conservatively, and I liked it.

A far cry from the girl she'd once been. But I'd liked her then, too.

"A piano bar," I said, bringing my thoughts back to the present, rather than the past.

"Well, I wasn't expecting this on a date."

I cringed. "Too much? We can go out to eat. Dillon didn't sound too excited when I mentioned only dinner, so I changed my mind."

A smile broke out on her face, and the light in her eyes danced a little.

"You asked Dillon for help?" she prodded, and I sighed.

"Yeah. Apparently, that kid knows how to help others when it comes to dating. He helped his brothers, and I was desperate."

"Desperate?"

I had no idea what to think about that word. She hadn't put any emotion into it, and I was worried.

"I, uh…" I trailed off then slid my hand through my hair and squeezed her hand with my other one. "Okay. I'm really not good at this. I wanted to make sure this was fun for you and not stupid and boring, so I asked Dillon because, sometimes, he knows what he's doing. Or all the time. I'm not really sure how. The kid has magic or something."

"Yeah, he does. I'm glad you asked him. It's kind of nice. And the idea of a piano bar is great. I love music."

"I know."

She looked at me then and kept smiling, but there was something different in her eyes now. Something I couldn't quite read.

"I don't know how to play the piano," she said softly.

"Oh. Well, you don't need to know how to play to come here. I have a reservation for seven, though. We should get in."

"That sounds great. This is nice, Beckham. Thanks for inviting me."

"You're welcome." I let out a sigh and shook my head. Maybe I wasn't completely terrible at this. I let go of her hand and brushed my thumb across her cheek. I watched her eyes darken, and I prayed I was doing the right thing.

"I hope you have fun tonight."

"I have a feeling I will."

"Good."

"It's lovely in here," Meadow said, looking around the place as we sat in the corner near the dais. The bar had dark lighting, with a gorgeous piano in the corner where Sam, the resident player, sang and did his thing.

"I come here every so often. I like the people."

"And it's a little bit different than the bar you work at."

"Yeah, that, too. I love the Connolly Brewery. I love what it is and what they stand for and the people. It's a great place. But, sometimes, it's fun to do something a little different."

She looked at me then as if searching for something on my face. I hoped she found it. Though I had no idea what it could be. "I like that, too."

"Hey, Beck, you going to play for us tonight?" Sam asked into the microphone, and everyone looked over. I could feel the tips of my ears turn red, and Meadow looked at me, her eyes wide.

"You play?" she asked, grinning. "Really?"

"A little."

"What do you say? Ask your girl there. I'm sure she'd love you to play."

"Beck! Beck!" The others weren't screaming it, just a few regulars saying my name as others started to look over and smile.

Damnit. I hadn't expected this.

"Maybe another time," I grumbled, trying to sound nice.

This was a damn classy place, after all, and I was on a date. Maybe I had made the wrong move bringing Meadow here.

"You should play."

"Not tonight." I looked over at her, trying to show her what I was thinking. Not that I knew what that was exactly.

"I'd like to see you play sometime."

"Maybe our next date."

She raised a brow. "So we're going on another date?" she asked.

I let my cocky side out because it was easier to be that guy than the one who had no idea what he was doing. I grinned and leaned back in the booth as I reached forward a bit to brush my fingertips along hers. She didn't pull her hand away. I counted that as progress.

"Yeah, I'm pretty sure it's already in the cards."

"Like I said, I have no idea how you can get through life with that ego of yours."

If she only knew.

"I do okay."

"I'm sure."

The waitress came, and we ordered our drinks, me a water with a whiskey neat. She got the same.

"You like whiskey?" I asked, and she smiled.

"Sometimes. I like to try everything. At least, when I was younger. I had to try everything. Almost all at once. Now, I like to do a little at a time."

That was the first time she'd ever mentioned her life before now, before meeting me. And I wanted to count that as progress, too. Only I didn't know if she would ever open up fully.

If she did, I would have to come clean as well. And I worried she wouldn't forgive me.

"How did you start working for the Connollys?" she asked later as we were both sipping our whiskeys and waiting for our meals.

"I showed up one day. Saw a *Help Wanted* sign in the window and got the job."

"That's it?"

I shrugged, playing with the condensation on my glass. "Yeah. Just like that. I needed a job. They needed a bartender. And I'm the best."

"Ego."

I tilted my head, smirking at her a bit. "You like it."

She paused and smiled. "Maybe."

There. That was the spark. She didn't always hide, there was a lick of fire within her that called to me. One that showed the girl she had been. I knew neither of us was the person we had been before. And that was fine. We didn't need to be. But that fire, that spark, *that* told me she was better than she was before. That she was okay.

And that's all I needed to know. All I wanted.

"How did you start out in your job?"

"My job's boring."

"Not really."

She raised a brow. "Sure. Whatever you say."

"Okay, so I would suck at it, but you do it. And you look like you have fun doing it. Why call it boring?"

"Most people think it is. I know it's not *that* boring. Or at least it's not to me. I got started in it because it was my favorite subject in school. Science. All of the sciences. And when I was in community college and working full-time, one of my professors needed help with something, so I got another job helping him. It didn't pay much, but it was fun to learn all the ins and outs of writing a textbook. One thing led to another, and suddenly, it was a career. It's not huge, and I'm not a multimillionaire or anything, but I do okay."

"Yeah, you do."

She smiled then, and it reached her eyes. I felt like I was on top of the world. Like I had finally done something right.

We ate our dinners—steak and baked potatoes and crisp green beans for me, chicken in her case. It was nice to simply be and enjoy the music and the ambiance. It wasn't something I did often.

This place was far removed from my life before. There were no screaming people in the corner, no drugs, no one practically having sex on the bar. There were no dangerous moves or the idea that you could die if you took the wrong step. Not that we were always that dramatic, but sometimes, it felt like that.

There was no stepping on one another to make sure you were the best.

This was a place to…be.

And I liked who I was with.

When I took Meadow home, and we talked about nothing except for our friends and our jobs, I figured this was possibly the best first date I'd ever been on. The only real first date.

"This was nice," she said, grinning. "Really nice."

"You sound surprised," I said, grinning a bit as we stood on her porch.

"Maybe. I didn't know what this would be."

"And what is this?" I asked, the words out of my mouth before I'd even fully thought them.

"I don't know exactly."

She went up on her tiptoes and kissed me square on the mouth.

My eyes widened, and I reached around, holding her close as I kissed her back.

She tasted of whiskey and our dinner. And Meadow. I wanted to kiss her harder, to push her against the door and have my way with her until we both came, but I knew that wasn't the right move. It would be a horrible idea.

"Jesus," I drawled, pulling myself back before I pushed her against the door and slid my hand down her pants like I wanted to. I was better than this. I had to be. She deserved more than a quick fuck against a door. She deserved everything. She had, even before, and she sure as hell did now.

"Thank you for dinner," she whispered, licking her wet lips.

"Yeah. We need to do that again."

"The kiss?" she asked, her eyes dancing.

"Dinner, the kiss…everything."

"As long as you promise to play for me."

"Maybe. But you're going to have to kiss me again first."

And then I slammed my mouth down on hers, not able to hold back.

She wrapped her arms around my neck, and I growled as I kissed her, our tongues sliding against one another.

"We need to stop," I rasped.

She pulled back, looking into my eyes, and I saw that spark again, the flame that reminded me of who she had been, mixed with the girl I knew now.

"What if we don't?" she whispered, and I froze.

"Are you sure?" I asked, my voice barely coming out through my clenched teeth. This couldn't be happening. This had to be some fantasy I'd thought up. Maybe a dream. It couldn't be real.

But I held her in my arms, and I knew it *was* real. So damn real.

"Yeah. But no promises. Okay? Just make me feel."

"That I can do." And then my mouth was on hers again, and her hands were on my back.

I pulled away long enough for her to get her keys out of her purse, and then we were inside, the door closed behind us. I watched as she flipped each lock, making sure we were safe inside. I didn't resent her for that time. I hated that she felt she had to be that careful, but I was glad for it all the same.

"You have to be sure," I said again, asking her to reassure us both. "Because as much as you say I have that big ego, I'm not going to take advantage of you."

She looked at me then, and slid her pin out of her hair, the strands falling in luscious waves down her back and chest.

"Yes…" A pause. "Yes." This time firmer.

"I don't know if I can be gentle," I whispered, running my hands down her face. "And I think you need gentle, baby girl."

"No. I don't think I need it to be too gentle. For now, let's just be you and me. No past. No future. Only us. It's what I need. Okay?"

I studied her face and nodded before kissing her again.

She was so soft beneath me, a moan sliding through her lips as I kissed her harder.

I pulled away, only long enough for her to lead me to the bedroom. I looked around her house, noticing small details as we passed, like the fact that she didn't have any photos on the walls of people, only some of landscapes, places she might've been or perhaps some that didn't mean anything at all.

But then my mouth was on hers again as we entered her bedroom, and I noticed the big bed behind her.

I couldn't wait to see her splayed out, to join her.

There were no words then, none were needed.

I lowered my head, slowly running my lips along her jaw before easing her coat off her body. It slid to the floor, and then I latched my mouth onto her neck, softly biting down as she groaned, turning her head slightly so I had better access.

"You're so fucking beautiful," I growled out.

"I need to come," she whispered.

I grinned. And then I was kissing her harder, stripping her out of her clothes as quickly as I could. I was so rock-hard beneath my jeans that I was afraid I might blow right then. There was no need to be gentle. I didn't think either of us needed that right then.

What I needed was for this to be her and me, only us, but not too much so. I had to be able to walk away. Being able to run to keep her safe was important. And I couldn't do that if I was too invested.

I pushed those thoughts out of my head and lived in the moment.

I eased her onto the bed and my mouth on hers, slowly working her bra off as I did. Her tits were big enough to fill my hands, her rose-colored nipples tight and puckered into hard little buds. I sucked one into my mouth, and she moaned.

"Beckham," she groaned out.

"That's it, let me taste you."

I kissed up and down her body, helping her out of her pants. She wiggled beneath me.

And when I worked my way down her front, I grinned at her black, lace thong and had to hold back a groan of my own. She was so fucking beautiful. All curves and softness. She had a few tattoos, a handful of scars, and I knew where those had come from, but I wasn't going to say anything.

There didn't need to be words.

When I kissed her over her panties, she arched beneath me, her hands sliding through my hair.

I was glad that my beard had grown back because it was getting long enough that it was turning soft. I slowly rubbed my cheeks along the insides of her thighs, and she pressed her legs together around my shoulders, arching under me.

"Beckham."

I grinned and slowly slid her panties out of the way, looking at her wet folds before latching on to her clit. I sucked, licked, then used a finger to tease her entrance.

She moaned, writhing under me, but I kept sucking, kept licking. And when she tightened around my finger, her body arching, I kept going, easing her through her orgasm until she was right on the edge again.

She tugged at my hair as I pulled away, and I grinned.

"I need to be inside you," I growled out.

"Beckham."

Apparently, that was all she could say, and I was totally fine with that.

"You're so beautiful when you come."

"Nice words. But I don't see you doing anything else."

"Feisty. I like it."

"I'd like it if you weren't dressed while I'm lying here naked beneath you."

She reached for the buckle of my belt, but I pushed her hand away. "You touch me, I'm going to blow right now. And I have a reputation to uphold."

She raised a brow and then cupped her breasts. "Really?"

That was the Meadow I liked. One that could be herself. Fuck. She was so fucking sexy. "Okay, no. But play with me anyway."

I pulled my shirt off over my head and then undid my belt, moving back so I could strip out of the rest of my clothes.

I pulled a condom from my pants' pocket, knowing I had put it there just in case, though hoping she didn't think that I assumed we would be doing this tonight.

Better safe than sorry, though. Right?

She didn't say anything, her eyes dark as she watched me slowly roll the condom over my length.

I cupped my balls, squeezing the base of my dick as I looked at her, and I knew if I weren't careful, I wasn't going to make it inside her.

And I really wanted to be inside her.

She licked her lips, and I crawled over her, slowly positioning myself at her entrance.

"You ready?"

"Always."

And then I slammed into her. One thrust, and I was balls-deep.

She screamed my name, and I captured her shout with my mouth.

Her legs locked around my waist, and even as she adjusted to my girth, I slowly pumped in and out of her, increasing my speed as I did.

Her fingernails raked down my back as I slammed into her, one thrust, then another.

I wanted to fuck her hard into the mattress, wanted to show her exactly who I once was, even though I knew I shouldn't.

And because of that thought, I twisted around, moving to my back with her on top as I slid my hands over her hips.

"Ride me."

She raked her fingers through her hair before putting both hands on her breasts, pinching her nipples.

"If you say so." And then she rocked her hips, rolling as she rode my cock.

"Fuck," I growled, gripping her hips tightly so she could sit still for a minute.

"Too good?" she asked, licking her lips.

"Fuck yeah." And then I fucked her. Rising up and down so quickly, the sounds I made echoed in my ears. It made things that much hotter.

She lowered over me, kissing me as I tugged on her hair and fucked her hard.

I slid one hand between us, flicking my thumb over her clit, and she came. When she clamped around me, I pumped once, twice, and then I came with her, whispering her name into her mouth as I kissed her.

I couldn't hold back, didn't want to.

So we kept moving, even as both of us came down from our orgasms.

I wanted more but knew I couldn't take it. Was positive I couldn't give it.

And as she looked at me, I saw the girl she'd been before, and I knew I felt like the guy I'd once been as well.

But then I saw the scars, the ones on her body I could see, and the ones I couldn't. And I thought about the ones she couldn't see on me.

And not only the visible ones that reminded me of who we were. The ones inside, as well.

Though this had been the best night of my life, I knew it couldn't last.

Because she was a princess. And I was the bastard who'd worked with her ex-boyfriend.

I was the asshole who hadn't known all the horrors of what had happened with her until it was too late.

I was that bastard. And she would always be the princess.

And when she found out who I was? Who I had been back then?

There'd be nothing left.

Just like I deserved.

Chapter 6

What is perfection?
Not my choices. But perhaps my reasons?
~Meadow, journal entry

Meadow

Apparently, I could figure out what normal was if I really tried. Or this was my normal, and I was okay with it. "Really? I can't believe you like scallops." I shuddered as Beckham rolled his eyes, tossing the shrimp into the scampi.

"Scallops are amazing. They're like butter."

"Then eat butter."

He raised a brow at me, shaking his head.

Now I loved it when he smirked. Yes, it was that ego that I always joked about with him. But it made me feel like I wasn't broken. And I really wasn't. I was okay. Sure, I was scared of my past, but I wasn't afraid of the people around me. Beckham didn't make me feel afraid.

"I'm not going to eat butter, weirdo."

"You're weird."

"Maybe. But I'm also cooking you dinner. I think that counts for something."

I shook my head and smiled at him.

We were four months into dating. Four months. I still couldn't believe we were doing this. We talked to each other every day, even if we didn't see each other. And when I went to the bar, he always grinned and winked at me as he helped fill orders, and then he'd make sure he kissed me firmly on the mouth later. In public. So everyone knew I was his.

Then again, in my mind, it was so everyone knew he was mine.

Not that I actually called him mine, because that would be a bit...much. We'd been very good about not assigning labels. We'd mentioned dating only since it was easy to say when we were going out together, but we did not say things like "boyfriend" or "girlfriend" or "lover" or anything like that.

That would make things scary. At least, in my mind.

I was probably overreacting, but I tended to do that.

But now, four months after our first date at the piano bar, I couldn't help but smile at him and feel like this was the normal that I'd craved. He still hadn't played for me yet, but one day soon, I knew he would. If I asked, he would. And I didn't know what to do with that kind of trust.

I hadn't heard from my mom or anyone else from my past since Mom stopped by months ago. And Beckham acted as if this was our life now.

I loved it.

Now he was here, in my home, making me dinner. I knew he would spend the night. And I would wake up in the morning curled in his arms before he slid into me, and we woke each other coming and calling each other's names.

It was odd to think that it had happened so quickly, and yet not fast enough.

I didn't think of Coby anymore. Yes, Beckham had tattoos and marks on his body like Coby did, but those scars were from an accident when he was younger—or so he said.

We didn't talk about that, though. We didn't discuss our pasts.

Perhaps that was my fault. Maybe it was his.

And it might get us into trouble one day. But that was fine. I only wanted to think about our present and our possible future. Even if it could lead us down two far different paths.

"You're looking all serious over there, cupcake." He leaned down and kissed me on the cheek.

"Cupcake?"

"I don't like calling you *baby* all the time. Makes it sound like I don't remember your name."

"You rarely call me Meadow."

"What am I supposed to call you? Flower?"

I shuddered.

"Now what's that look for?" Then he looked at me, a strange expression passing over his face as he shook his head. It was as if he knew that I didn't like being called that because it was too close to Petal, my mother's name. But he wouldn't know that. He couldn't. I hadn't mentioned my mom's name. And he didn't know her. He didn't know about my past.

I had to be seeing things.

"Anyway, I don't think *cupcake*'s the word you want to use. Now I'm hungry."

"I'm making you shrimp scampi, woman."

"Oh, good. Now, I'm going to be called *woman*. Great."

"Hey, better than cupcake."

"Now I *really* want cupcakes."

"How about this? After dinner, I'll head to the store and pick you up some cupcakes. How does that sound?"

I looked up at him then, and something made my heart clutch. It couldn't be that. Four months, and I had already pushed that aside. I could *not* fall in love with Beckham Masters.

I had fallen in love before, and it had screwed me over. Sure, this was completely different, and, no, I wasn't the same person as before. But I didn't want that. I couldn't have that.

I didn't know what would happen to him if I had to leave. If my past came after me again. Or if he found out who I was. Who I had been before. What would he think of me?

Would he still want me?

I couldn't fall in love with him. But I could have him for now. That would have to be enough.

"I think after dinner, we should be just fine. Plus, I brought cheesecake." I grinned after I said it, batting my eyelashes, and he licked his lips.

Then I imagined him licking other places, and I went damp.

Dear God, the man turned me on so very quickly. It was a problem.

"Yeah? It's like you know I love cheesecake, woman."

"Stop calling me *woman*."

"Okay, cupcake."

"I'm going to kick your ass."

"Oh, you can try. But don't worry, I can take you."

"So you say. But all I have to do is strip naked, and then you'll be at my mercy."

He flipped the scampi a bit on the stove before removing it from the heat and leaning against the counter. And then he folded his arms over his chest and raked his gaze down my body. I could practically feel him touching me. My nipples hardened, and my panties got wet.

Dear God, Beckham was so damned good at that. He was an addiction.

Definitely my weakness.

"Well, why don't we try it out? You strip down and get naked, and I'll try to take you."

"After dinner."

"So no cheesecake, then?"

"I'm sure we can work the cheesecake in somehow," I said, laughing. He reached around, gripped me by my ass, and lifted me up.

He set me on the counter, and I wrapped my legs around his waist.

"The dinner's going to get cold if we don't start eating."

"I'm thinking about something else I'd rather eat," he said and bit down on my lower lip.

When he licked away the sting, I leaned my head back so he could move his lips down and suck on my throat.

I loved when he caressed my neck.

I hadn't always liked it because I remembered the last time someone had touched my neck—with their hands. And not in a good way. Coby had tried to choke me before my mother came in, yelling about something or other.

I still didn't know if she'd wanted him to stop, or if something elsewhere had needed his or my attention.

He'd only choked me that once.

Before that, I hadn't had a problem with anyone touching my neck.

But now when Beckham did it? It wasn't the same. I didn't feel that fear. It felt…perfect.

I really shouldn't think that word.

Things couldn't be perfect.

When they felt that way, that's when things got scary.

"Let's eat dinner first," I whispered, pushing him away slightly. If he took me now, I was afraid I would be lost forever.

And we needed some distance.

I couldn't fall for him. Couldn't let him know about my past.

Even though I desperately wanted to know about his. There had to be boundaries.

No matter what, we needed those lines that we didn't cross.

"Okay. You're so mean to me."

I shoved at his chest as he helped me down from the counter.

"I'm sorry, you big baby."

"Let's eat quickly. I need to get inside you, woman."

"I'm going to take my time then, *cupcake*."

He raised a brow, and I chuckled, pulling down the plates so he could finish our meal.

We ate in the kitchen, both of us sitting at the counter as we laughed and talked about our days.

It was nice. Normal. But I couldn't let it become routine. Just in case things got too comfortable. If they did, I feared we'd both end up hurting. But if we kept things as they were, nothing permanent, and ordinary enough that it didn't feel weird, I figured that was an excellent middle ground.

Not that I knew if we were actually on the right side of the line we'd drawn.

"So we going for the cheesecake now? Or are we going to watch that movie we talked about? Or are you thinking about being my dessert?"

I shook my head, taking his plate and bringing it to the sink.

"How about we do dinner and cheesecake?"

He frowned, leaning forward to kiss me on my forehead.

"Anything you want, babe. You feeling okay?"

"Yes. I'm fine. Just a little tired, I think."

He looked at me then, reaching around to knead my butt. I loved when he did that. He was always so gentle, but constantly touching me.

I hadn't known he'd be like this. Oh, I'd had a feeling that Beckham would be possessive, but I hadn't known he would be so sweet. There was a huge difference between the way he was with me and how Coby had been.

I really needed to stop comparing them. There was no comparison. "Do you want me to head home?" he asked, frowning as he studied my face. I shook my head.

"No, let's watch the movie. I'm not caught up on all the *Avengers* yet."

"Then I feel like I've failed you."

"You know, I think that's exactly what Dillon said when I mentioned it at the bar."

"Well, Dillon's the one who made sure I watched them in the correct order, not chronological, but how they were released theatrically as intended by the original filmmakers."

"Please don't get on another *Avengers* rant," I said, shaking my head even as I laughed.

"Hey, it's been like three, maybe four days since I went on a rant about the *Avengers*."

"More like three or four minutes."

He smiled. "Okay, honey, whatever you say."

I raised a brow. "Really?"

"Hey, I called you *honey*. It's better than cupcake."

"No, it's really not. Just call me Meadow."

"I like calling you everything."

He looked at me then, and I swallowed hard. Then I took a few steps back, feeling afraid.

So damned scared.

He had to stop looking at me like that. Needed to stop treating me like I was so precious. Because it felt too good. It felt like forever, and that was something I couldn't give him. Or myself.

He was so good, so sweet. But he didn't have my past. Didn't have the connections I did. What happened when Coby got out of jail, or someone from his club figured out exactly where I was? What would happen to Beckham then? Being with me wasn't good for him. I had to make it easy for him to walk away. I had to make it simple. For him? For me? I didn't know. But I at least had to try.

"Come on, let's watch that movie, and then we'll have dessert. Even if it's only our own." I winked as I said it, and he groaned, then gave my ass a squeeze before slapping it.

"I'll help you with dishes, pretty lady."

"*Pretty lady* makes you sound like a cowboy."

"Hey, you're the one who rode me last."

I winced at his horrible joke, and then kissed him again before doing the dishes.

This was normal. Everything was fine.

But it couldn't mean anything more than it already did. If it did start to mean more, I'd hurt him in the end. And myself. And I'd already broken once. I was afraid that if I had to walk away, or when Beckham did, I would end up shattered. In a far different way, yet still the same as before. I didn't want to be that Meadow anymore. I didn't think I *could* be.

But one look at Beckham, and I was afraid he'd see that old me.

Even if it truly broke me in the end.

Chapter 7

Beckham

I looked over at Meadow dancing in the corner of the bar with the girls and couldn't hold back my smile. She seemed so damn *happy*.

And the hell of it was, I was happy, too.

That's why I hadn't told her that I knew about her past.

Why I didn't tell her anything about mine.

I was the worst kind of coward.

But I didn't know how to reveal those things without ruining what we had. Even if I knew that what we had couldn't be fully realized until I did.

Jesus, I was a horrible person.

"Why the long face?" Dillon asked as he sidled up to me behind the bar. He started helping me clean the dirty glasses, and I shrugged.

"No reason."

"Yeah. Not buying that. If you want to talk, just let me know."

"You're a good kid."

Dillon glanced over at me, his hands covered in suds. "Thanks. But I'm not really a kid anymore."

"Well, since we're your elders, you're always going to be a kid to us."

"That's what Cameron says. Maybe when I'm actually allowed to drink behind the bar, I won't be a kid anymore."

"Well, first, you don't drink behind the bar."

"You know what I mean. Actually be legal to drink rather than just standing here, helping you clean glasses."

"Hate to break it to you, kid," I said with a wink, "but your family and I are probably always going to call you that. Even when we're all in our fifties."

"So that means you're going to be here until then?" Dillon asked, his voice suddenly serious.

I looked at him, trying to figure out what I should say. I didn't have an answer. Did I want to be? Yeah, maybe. And that was the first time I'd really let myself think that. I hadn't allowed myself to think anything like that before. I wanted to stay. I liked what I had here. I enjoyed this feeling. I loved being happy. But everything could change in an instant. It had already changed more than once in my life. And I knew I couldn't let myself get too settled. Forget where I came from. But I didn't say any of that. Instead, I shrugged and looked over at Dillon.

"That'd be nice, wouldn't it?"

"Maybe." Dillon smiled as he said it, and I had a feeling he was trying to lighten the mood since things felt kind of heavy right then.

He was a good kid, a good man. And I had a feeling as he grew up, he would grow into an even better one.

I liked him. Cared about all the Connolly brothers. And even though I worked for them, they made me feel like I was a part of their family.

Not a bad deal.

"Okay, you're off, right?" Ben asked as he came up and nodded at one of the customers before pulling a draft. "Go hang out with your girl. They're all dancing in the corner, and I think the Connollys over there want you to play pool."

"They just want me to kick their asses," I said, winking.

"Don't let Brendon hear you say that. He and Harmony still hold the record. I mean, it was only one tourney, but it's still the record."

"For now."

"Yes, for now," Aiden said as he came out with two plates of food in his hands. He set them down on the bar, nodded at Big Ben, and gestured for us to follow him.

"You know the only reason that Brendon and Harmony won that pool tournament is because Sienna and I weren't there," Aiden said, shaking his head.

I gave Dillon a look. He smirked, and then we both just shook our heads, holding back laughter. Oh, we knew why the two of them hadn't been at that final pool tournament round. Aiden and Sienna had been doing something of their own. Not that we'd mention that. Especially when everybody could hear us, and Sienna could probably kick my ass.

Okay, there was no *probably* about it. She *would* kick my ass. And Meadow wouldn't like that.

Meadow.

I looked over at her, and she smiled, the warmth in her eyes pulling me in.

Damn. I was falling for her. I knew I shouldn't. It wasn't safe. But I was pretty sure I had already fallen. I'd probably started at the wedding. Maybe even before that.

I shouldn't have danced with her. Shouldn't have done so much.

"Okay, come on over," Cameron said from the corner. "Pool table's ours for the next hour. Let's play." He twirled his finger in the air, and Violet rolled her eyes before going and kissing her man on the mouth.

He grinned down at her and gripped her ass, and I shielded Dillon's eyes, even as the kid laughed.

"Hey. There are sweet, innocent eyes over here. Don't scar him."

"Innocent?" Dillon asked, and I glared down at him.

"Excuse me, my baby brother is a perfect, lily-white virgin," Brendon shouted, and the tips of Dillon's ears turned red.

Either the kid was embarrassed about his brothers yelling, or Dillon actually *was* a virgin. Considering that I had seen him with more than one girl over the time I'd known him, I had a feeling Dillon was no virgin. However, having your brothers discuss your sex life—or lack thereof—really loudly in the bar that you visited almost daily probably wasn't the best thing in the world.

"Please, stop," Dillon grumbled.

"Oh, be nice," Harmony said, wrapping her arms around Dillon. "It's kind of nice that he stays sweet and innocent. I mean, it's tough to find that these days. Just know that you're special to us. We love you." She kissed him on the brow, and I saw the laughter in her eyes even as everyone else actually broke out in fits of giggles and cheers.

Dillon narrowed his eyes at her, but he didn't say anything. Nobody could ever be mean to Harmony.

She was sneaky like that. I liked it.

Meadow slid to my side, and I wrapped my arm around her shoulders. "They sure do love teasing him," Meadow said, and I shrugged, even as I pulled her closer.

"Yeah, but he gives as much as he gets. It's kind of nice having a family that makes fun of each other and yet will always be there for one another."

"I know. Sometimes, I'm a little jealous. They're just so good for each other. You know?" I nodded but didn't look down at her. I knew her old man. And that guy would never be there for her. For anyone. He only cared about his club and himself. And not in that order.

I knew he didn't give a damn about his little girl. Hadn't before, and sure as hell didn't now. At least for more than what she could do for him.

And, honestly, I wasn't even sure he cared about his old lady.

But that had to stay in the past. We needed to think about the present. And maybe the future.

As Meadow went quiet and introspective beside me, I knew she was thinking about her family as well.

We really weren't very good at this. I needed to tell her. It wasn't fair of me to keep these secrets.

I might lose her in the end by opening up, but lying to her wasn't the answer.

I would tell her tomorrow. Telling her tonight while we were with friends would ruin the evening. Maybe that was the coward's way out, but I figured that telling her tomorrow would work. It had to. I only hoped I didn't ruin everything by doing it. I hoped I didn't lose it all when I opened up. But this wasn't about me. I needed to remember that. I had made my choices, my own decisions.

And I wasn't going to turn away from that. Not now. Not when I was starting to feel what I did for her. It wasn't fair. Not to either of us. But mostly, not to her.

"Okay, now that we have completely embarrassed the kid—good job, family—it's time to get going," Aiden said as he looked over at his woman. "Watch while Sienna and I kick all of your asses."

"That's my man," she said before taking a sip of her beer.

"The competition gets a little weird with all of you guys together," I said.

"That is true." Violet looked over at Dillon.

"I thought you were bringing one of your roommates to play."

Dillon shook his head. "No, and I can't stay either. Homework."

"Well, I'm glad you were here for a bit. And I'm happy you're putting your studies first." She leaned down and kissed the top of Dillon's head since he had taken one of the seats near the pool table.

She had started becoming almost motherly to him lately, and I had a feeling Dillon liked it, even if there wasn't a huge age gap between any of them.

"Okay, then, I guess it's just four teams. Two pool tables, four teams, let's see who wins."

Sienna clapped her hands, and our mini pool tournament started.

An hour later, my gut hurt from laughing, my pride stung from the fact that we were in fourth place, and all I could do was look at Meadow, who grinned.

"I'm not always bad at pool," Meadow said. "Actually, I'm usually pretty good."

"It probably doesn't help that you guys are pinching each other's asses while you're playing," Aiden said dryly.

"It's true," Sienna said. "We try not to distract each other with sex when we're playing."

"Really?" I said, deadpan. "Aren't you the two that practically humped back there in the storage room?"

Sienna blushed. "I have no idea what you're talking about, Beckham. I am utterly sweet and innocent."

Everyone laughed so hard, I was pretty sure that Sienna was going to hit us all with her pool cue. But she didn't.

Meadow had just set up her shot when a voice from behind us made me freeze. My balls shrank, my back turned to stone, and I swallowed hard. I hoped to hell it wasn't who I thought it was. But I knew it was. I knew exactly who the fuck it was.

"Hey, what do we have here?"

No one else seemed to notice the tension in the air. They didn't know who was now in their midst. And why should they? They didn't know who I was at my core, and they sure as hell didn't know where Meadow had come from. They did not know these people. I'd hoped to hell they never would. Unfortunately, that didn't seem to be the case.

I turned. There was no use hiding. There was no way I could run. They'd find me. They always did.

Cliff's eyes widened for a fraction of a second, and that's when I knew they weren't here for me. No, they had simply come in, and they'd found me.

"Just a friendly pool game. We're almost done if you want the tables," I said, my voice casual. The Connollys must have figured out that there was something wrong because they all stood a little straighter and angled their bodies so they stood in front of their women. I knew that they didn't know exactly what was going on. Then again, *I* didn't really know.

"Beckham," Cliff growled out. "I knew you were around here. At least, somewhere in the city. Had to be. You wouldn't go too far since you're a lazy fuck. Always were. It's my luck that I was the one to find you."

"We don't want any trouble here. We're just playing pool. I'm only the bartender."

Meadow stiffened beside me. I hated this. Fuck. I couldn't take her to the side and explain things to her now, tell her why I had kept my past a secret. It was over. She would likely hate me forever. I had to get these guys out of here before they recognized who was standing beside me. If I weren't careful, they would figure it out. And I didn't know what would happen if they did. It wasn't safe for Meadow. I shouldn't have stayed as long as I did. I shouldn't have even become her friend. But I had. And now, she wasn't safe.

"Sure," Cliff said, "but maybe we should go out back and talk. It's been a long time since we've seen you, Beck. I see you're just as ugly as ever with that fucking beard of yours. Couldn't even grow it. Had to be a patchy-assed-face like usual."

"Hey, this is our bar. If you're going to start something, you should leave. We don't take kindly to violence here," Cameron said, his voice low but still a growl.

Cliff looked over at him and snorted. "Okay, pretty boy. Whatever you say. We don't want no trouble either. Just surprised to see Beck is all. And acting all casual, like he isn't the scum of the earth. A fucking traitor."

I stiffened then and slowly angled my body a little bit more so they couldn't see Meadow. Thankfully, none of the guys in front of me looked toward her. And even better, the woman beside them wasn't looking.

I knew her. Trace. Coby's sister, his damn twin.

And, if I remembered right, she was Cliff's old lady. But that had been a while ago, and even though you didn't poach women—one of the primary rules of being a brother—things happened.

But hell, things were getting a little too intense. I needed to get them out of here and away from Meadow.

"I don't want any trouble. I'm out. You know that."

The Connollys all looked at each other, and I could see them out of the corner of my eye, but I ignored them. They weren't the dangerous ones. No, the guys in front of me were.

The ones who ran drugs and did shit that I wasn't proud of.

They weren't like some who dealt in guns and other things. But they were the worst of the bunch.

And I'd brought them right to my friends' door. Sure, they might not have known that I was here when they walked in, but now they were trying to start something because I was.

I needed to make it stop.

"Come on, guys, you don't need to do this."

"Yeah, maybe we do," Cliff growled. I noticed that the others didn't say anything, but they didn't need to. With Coby in jail, Cliff was number one outside of the main circle.

Coby had been the leader of his generation. And I'd followed him. Of course, then I'd become VP over him, and everything changed. Things had gotten worse. Coby found a woman, even though I hadn't known who she was at the time.

Coby always wanted more power. Because I didn't like the man I'd become, I left.

It hadn't been easy. And I bled for it in the end, burned for it.

I'd left, and Coby took my place. And Coby had gone to jail because of his own stupidity.

I hadn't paid for my crimes. And I knew Cliff, Coby's BFF, blamed me for that.

"Hey, I have the cops on the line, and I can get them here at any minute. So why don't you guys get out?"

I held back a curse as Sienna spoke, and I had a feeling the rest of the Connollys did, too.

"You really going to let your bitch talk for you?" Cliff asked, and I moved forward, putting my hands on his colors. The leather felt soft and supple under my palms, but I twisted it until it cracked.

"Just go. You don't have any business here. This isn't your place. This isn't some TV show where you can fuck up a bar because you feel like it. Just go before you end up in jail again like your little buddy. You hear me? You're not wanted here."

Cliff's eyes narrowed, but when one of the other guys elbowed him in the side, I pulled away. Cliff growled at me.

"Come on. You're on probation, man."

"Come on, Cliff. I'm tired of this already. Let's just go home," Trace whined, leaning into her man.

I ignored the other guy, my eyes on Cliff.

"This isn't over, Beck."

"It was over a long time ago, and we both know it. Go back to the life you chose. I'm making mine here."

"For now, asshole."

"No. Forever. Just go."

The guys grumbled, and I had a feeling it had nothing to do with my words. No, it was because of the men at my back and the fact that the rest of the bar had gone silent, even though some of our regulars, big men in their own rights, had also stood up, ready to do what they could to help.

Only five minutes in, and the guys had made this place a biker bar. One where there'd be a fight and blood and broken glass.

And it would all be my fucking fault.

The members of my old club turned on their heel and left, but not before knocking down a couple of chairs and cursing up a storm as they did.

Glass shattered on the floor as they knocked into one of the tables, but no one moved to pick it up. At least not right away.

The others started talking, asking me questions, wanting to know what was happening, but I couldn't listen. I didn't have eyes for them. No, I could only look at the woman at my side, who hadn't said a word. The one who didn't want to draw attention to herself. And I knew why.

I looked over at Meadow, my jaw tight as I tried to open my mouth to say something. But there were no words.

She simply looked at me, her eyes wide as she blinked. "You knew them. You're part of them." Her voice was so hollow, like the one I'd heard when I first met her. Not the Meadow she was now.

"Yeah. No use in lying. I was." I paused. I knew I shouldn't say the rest, but realized I probably needed to. "It was before you were part if it with Coby, though."

Her face blanched, and she took a staggering step back. "You knew. You knew?"

The others looked at us, confusion clear on their faces, but I had to ignore them.

"Yeah. I did."

I was prepared for the slap, ready for the shove, the punch, something.

But I didn't expect what actually happened.

She looked at me, took another step back, and then turned on her heel, grabbed her bag, and walked out.

I looked over at Cameron and gestured towards her. "Can you follow her? Make sure that the others don't find her. She wouldn't welcome my help."

"Yeah, we got it," Cameron said, his voice low. "But then you're going to explain exactly what the fuck just happened."

"Promise. Just make sure she's safe."

"I'll go, too," Aiden said, following Cameron.

And then the two were off to make sure Meadow got home okay in case the guys were out there waiting.

I wanted to be there. I wanted to fix this. But I didn't think I could.

I looked at Brendon and the girls, and I swallowed hard. I didn't know what to say, so I didn't say anything.

Instead, I picked up the chair and went to get a broom to sweep up the glass.

I figured if it was my last day at the Connolly Brewery, I might as well clean up some of the mess I'd indirectly made.

But I also knew that, no matter what, some messes couldn't be cleaned up. Some stains would forever haunt the place.

Just as they hung over me.

Chapter 8

Imperfections breed doubt. Or is it the other way around?
~Meadow, journal entry

Meadow

My fingers slid over the tattoo on my ribcage, the other on my hip, the morning light casting shadows along my skin. They were flowers and vines, two inconspicuous tattoos that had been for me, not for anyone else.

The one on my other hip, however, had been lasered off.

I had been stupid and young and not even eighteen when I had Coby's name tattooed on my hip. He'd asked me to put it there, wanted his name on my flesh where no one else could see. That way, I would know I was his property. That I was always his.

I could still see the scar, the marks. But I couldn't see his name. And that had been enough for me. It had been healing.

Because I no longer bore the name of the man I'd thought I loved but who really only wanted to own me. Instead, I boasted the scars of my decisions, not ones of ownership.

Beckham had seen my tattoos, my scars. But he hadn't said anything.

Had he known that Coby's name had been on my hip? Had he realized that the mark had been erased by a laser because I was ashamed of where I came from? Or the fact that I had actually done it so I could become myself rather than who Coby wanted me to be?

Beckham had known. At least parts of it.

This entire time, he knew.

And I didn't know what to think about that.

He had been part of Coby's crew, although he'd said that he hadn't been part of it when I was there.

But Trace had been. Trace had always been Cliff's old lady, just like I had been Coby's.

And since Trace and Coby were twins, she had been my sister. In a weird sort of way that had nothing to do with love but rather ties that no one wanted to break. That others constantly told me could never be broken or severed.

I had hidden from her earlier at the bar, hadn't said a word, and that was my shame. Far beyond what Beckham had said, or what he had done, I carried the weight of my own decisions and truths.

I had hidden. I didn't want the others to know I was there.

I could blame part of that on shock. Surprise that they were at the bar and that they knew Beckham.

Shock that Beckham had known things about who I was and hadn't told me.

I curled my fists at my sides, trying to calm my breathing.

Why did it feel like such a betrayal? I hadn't been honest either.

And that was my issue.

I'd been to countless therapy sessions and yet I don't think I could pull anything from those to figure out the answers to why I hadn't been honest. I'd found my self-worth, but I hadn't been able to find my courage. Not all of it.

Beckham had known about me, but I hadn't known about him.

And neither of us had said anything.

We weren't truthful—not at all.

Instead, we had lived in this odd vacuum where we tried to make our own happiness that was pillowed on a cursed bed of lies.

While neither of us had said anything, Beckham had known about me, while I hadn't known about him.

But what was worse?

I didn't know, so I couldn't face him. I could barely face myself. But I was forcing myself to do that now.

I looked in the mirror one last time and then reached down to pull my shirt over my head.

I didn't need to look at my tattoos to know they were there. But I always did.

I didn't have to touch my scars to know that they existed on my body. Because they had been woven through my soul long before they were etched onto my skin.

And then I remembered the ink on Beckham's skin and the fact that I had touched every inch of him.

I remembered the scars beneath my fingertips, and I'd wondered where they came from, even though I had known they came from his past. Those scars had come from his club ink. The fact that it had been lasered off. Painfully. Perhaps even brutally. I hadn't realized how intertwined our paths had truly become.

And not only what was in front of us, but where we had come from as well.

"I don't know what I'm doing," I mumbled to myself and then shook my head. That seemed to be standard for me lately, and I *didn't* feel like I knew what I was doing. I hadn't spoken to anyone since I left, although Cameron and Aiden had walked me to my car. I'd smiled, nodded at them in thanks, and then driven home.

I'd locked the doors behind me, keeping my security system armed, and wondered if the club would find me.

Not that they were looking. No one knew where I was. And I hadn't thought my parents would mention it to anyone. Honestly, it wouldn't have done them any good. They only wanted me for money. And if I were pulled back into that life, I wouldn't have money for them.

So, maybe they were smarter than I gave them credit for.

The doorbell rang, and I looked over at it, frowning.

If it was Beckham, I didn't know what I would do. If it was someone else, someone from my past, I honestly didn't know what to do there either.

I looked down at my phone, at the camera on the security app, and let out a shuddering sigh of relief when I realized it was the girls.

I didn't know what I planned to say to them, though I knew I couldn't lie.

They would likely want to know why I ran, and not only because Beckham had come clean.

Plus, I didn't want to hide anymore. I was so tired of it. It just left me feeling like I was losing it when, sometimes, I felt like I didn't have much of *it* to begin with.

So I put my phone in my pocket and went to the front door, taking my time turning each lock as I did.

It was as if I were getting closer and closer to baring my soul with each snap of the lock, and I didn't know if I was strong enough to do it.

Violet, Harmony, and Sienna walked in, hugging me tightly as they did.

I smiled at them and then closed the door behind them, locking it tightly once more.

"Hi," I said, my voice soft.

"Hey," Harmony replied. "How are you feeling?"

"I'm okay. You guys didn't have to come over this morning."

"Yeah, we did," Violet said.

"And you need to tell us what happened. Maybe explain why you have those locks on your door. Why you looked so scared when those people came into the bar. And why you didn't look at any of them straight on. Oh, and why you ran."

Violet and Harmony glared at Sienna, and I shook my head, a smile playing on my face. Of course, Sienna would be the one to cut right to the chase. But they all had to wonder. And I was tired of lying. Of hiding.

"It's a little too early for wine, but I guess once I'm finished, you might want a glass. I know I will."

"You don't have to say anything you don't want to," Harmony said quickly. "And even though Sienna's the one that blurted that out, we didn't mean to come over here and make you feel like we were attacking you."

"Hey," Sienna said.

"Don't worry about it. I was thinking about how to tell you exactly what was going on anyway. You three coming over here made it easier for me and was so helpful.

"So, hi. My name's Meadow."

Sienna snorted. "Okay. We're going to start with that. We love you, you know?" she said quickly.

"Thanks." I let out a shuddering breath, my heart beating quickly even as my body warmed at that.

"We lost a friend because we didn't ask the right questions," Violet said softly. "And I know this is a completely different situation, but we're here for you. Okay?"

A tear slipped from her eye, and she quickly wiped it off her cheek. I nodded and then gestured for them to follow me into the living room.

"Let's sit down. I'll try to explain. Just don't hate me after, okay?" I added quickly.

"I don't think we could ever hate you, Meadow," Harmony said.

"You don't know who I was."

I thought about the scar on my hip, the ones on Beckham. And I knew that scars dug themselves in deeply. The path you traveled left evidence behind. I needed to figure out where I was at the end of my journey, so while the scars might remain, I would still be able to figure out what I needed to say.

"I knew the people that came in and recognized Beckham."

"Okay," Violet said. "Did you know that Beckham knew them?"

I shook my head. "Let me start from the beginning."

"We're here," Harmony said, reaching out and squeezing my hand. "We'll always be here."

And that's why I could say what I needed to. Why I could do this.

I'd never had friends like these before. The people in my old life hadn't been like this. Some in the club and on the periphery were able to form connections, but not me. I'd thought I had something with Coby, but that had been an unhealthy relationship that led to nothing but pain and heartache.

The girls in front of me deserved more. And I needed to be better for them.

So I'd tell them where I came from, *who* I'd been, and hopefully they could see who I was now.

Even if I wasn't always sure who that was.

"I knew them because I was one of them once upon a time."

"You were a biker?" Sienna asked incredulously, and I shrugged.

"That's part of the culture. I didn't have my own bike. I rode bitch. First behind my daddy when I was little, and then behind the boy I thought I'd fallen in love with."

"Oh," Violet said, looking at me wide-eyed.

"I know. That's not who I am now. But that's who I used to be. I grew up in the lifestyle. My dad was the president of an MC. And I thought it was the most amazing thing ever because while there're some TV shows and things that show MCs in a bad light with all the illegal crap and overdramatization, there are some beautiful clubs out there that give to charities and help with bullying and many amazing things. They're truly a family who do their best to make sure that the people in the club are taken care of. And they give back." I let out a shaky breath.

"When I was a little kid, that was ours. I don't know when it all changed. Maybe when I was about fourteen or so. But people needed money, and new blood came in. They started doing things they shouldn't. They weren't on the right side of the law anymore, and I knew there were drugs involved—only not as many as some other clubs." I let out a shaky breath, and the others looked at me.

"I'm sorry, Meadow," Harmony whispered.

"Me, too. But that's not the worst of it. As I mentioned, I met a boy. From a rival club. But it wasn't much of a rivalry, it was just an MC that was close by. Coby was the son of their president and wanted to be the vice president. I didn't really know much about it because it wasn't the club I grew up in. I fell for him hard. He was everything to me. I thought he loved me. And he treated me like I was the princess that everyone thought I was."

The girls looked at me, and I was grateful that they didn't say anything. It was hard enough getting this out as it was.

"My dad used to hit my mom. Not all the time, but enough that it scared me. But he'd always apologize, and they'd be fine afterwards. My mom would slap me and hit me and make me feel like crap and force me to think about my body in ways I shouldn't, especially as a way to get men. And so, when Coby treated me like a princess, I fell for it all. Then he hit me once, and then again, and I couldn't get out. The times I tried to leave, it was even worse."

"Oh, Meadow," Violet said. She moved forward to sit next to me on the couch, and I was grateful. The girls sat next to each other on the loveseat, holding each other's hands as they looked at me.

"Anyway, Coby and his club were even worse than my dad. They did so many horrible things. Mostly with drugs. And then I ratted them out." I let out a shaky laugh. "At least, I thought I did. Not completely, though. They didn't need my testimony to put Coby behind bars because they had enough evidence without it. They didn't even need me to get into the house. They didn't care that I was broken and bleeding when they found me."

"Are you serious?" Sienna asked, rage in her voice. "I'm so sorry."

"I don't know if that's actually the truth," I said quickly. "They might've cared, I don't know, but I was too hollow to process it. And I didn't tell them everything. There were things that they never needed to know. All I knew was that the incident gave me the out I needed. I left, and I didn't turn back. But my parents have always known where I am and constantly try to get money from me. That means anybody who blames me for what happened to Coby can find me."

I looked down at my hands.

"I didn't know Beckham was part of it. He wasn't in the club when I was there, but he knew my dad. He must have. He had to have known exactly who I was when we met."

"And he didn't say anything," Sienna whispered.

"No. And it's hard for me to completely blame him because I didn't tell him about my past either. I did horrible things when I was younger. Not anything illegal, but I wasn't who I am now. And I should have told him that. But he should've told me, too."

Tears were falling down my cheeks at that point, and the girls gathered around me, holding me close.

"It looked like he was out," Harmony whispered. "Maybe he didn't tell you because he didn't know how."

"That's no excuse," Violet said.

"I know. I'm just afraid. Afraid of what will happen if I let him in again. Because I thought I was out. I guess I was wrong."

Then the tears fell harder, and the girls simply held me.

I'd thought I was good at being boring. That was safe.

It'd kept me alive this long.

Alive.

But Beckham had been part of it all along, and I didn't know how to feel about that, even if he was out of the life.

I'd fallen once, and it had broken me.

I couldn't fall again.

I'd already paid that price.

This time, I was afraid it would cost even more.

"What are you going to do?" Sienna asked, and I shook my head.

"I don't know. He hasn't said anything to me."

"Maybe he's giving you space," Harmony said.

"Maybe. But I don't know what to say to him. He knew about my past."

"It sounds to me like he has even more baggage than you do, or at least an equal amount," Sienna lamented. "He got out. He wanted to put all of that behind him."

"I can understand that. And while I probably should have mentioned who I was to him, especially considering how long we've been together, he definitely should have mentioned that he knew me."

"Yes, he should have," Violet said, nodding. "And when he explains why he didn't, you can decide if you're willing to take him back or not."

"I can't. I can't take him back. What if the club finds him again?"

"I don't know, honey. But you're not alone now. You don't have your family, the ones that claim they raised you, but you do have us."

Harmony nodded tightly as she said it. "We are your family now. All of us. And no matter what, you can lean on us. I promise."

"I don't know what to say."

"Then don't say anything. You are allowed to have secrets. We won't pry. And we'll always be here for you—whenever you need us. So, here we are. For always." Violet kissed the top of my head. "Now, maybe we should have that wine, and you can tell us more if you want. Or we can talk about nothing. I don't mind either way. Regardless, we're not leaving you alone. We're here. Always."

I held on tight as the tears kept falling. I had a feeling that I was going to have to figure out exactly what to say to Beckham.

Because I knew more than anybody how hard it was to walk away from that life and try to pretend that you were normal.

But we had been brought together, and somehow, we needed to figure out what to do next.

Though I had a feeling that it wouldn't end the way I thought.

But what I had with Beckham *had* to end.

I couldn't do this again.

I *couldn't.*

Chapter 9

Beckham

I was wrapping up packing the rest of my duffle when someone's fist slammed on the door, and the doorbell rang a couple of times.

My spine stiffened, and I looked around for a weapon. Jesus Christ. Apparently, Cliff and Leonard had found me.

This was it. This was how it was going to end.

Because I didn't actually have a weapon on me, only a knife from the kitchen.

And I wasn't about to fight them.

I wasn't that man anymore. I talked my way out of issues. In the time since I'd left, putting my hands on Cliff's colors had been the only violent thing I'd done.

I refused to become that person again.

"Come on, Beck, open up."

My shoulders dropped as I realized who it was.

The Connollys. The Connollys were here.

Okay, then. I could do this. Maybe. The whole keeping my past a secret and lying to them thing probably wasn't the best. But I could deal.

At least, I hoped so.

They wouldn't hurt me too badly. Maybe.

I stuffed the last of my things into the duffle bag and made my way to the front door.

I opened it, and the Connollys barreled through. All four of them. Well, apparently, Dillon was going to be a part of this, too. Perfect.

"I see you told the kid."

Dillon raised a brow.

"You were almost in a biker fight in a bar. Of course they told me."

"Dillon," Cameron growled.

"What? I was worried. Can't I be worried?"

I glared at all of them.

"I already quit. I know I owe you all an explanation. But I don't know exactly what I need to say to you guys."

And that was the crux of it. I didn't know what to say. There was nothing that would put me in a good light. I didn't deserve that anyway.

"You don't get to quit," Aiden snarled. "And no, Beckham, we're not firing you either."

I could only look at them, blinking. "But I have to go. I can't stay."

"Because they'll find you?" Brendon asked, totally serious.

"I don't fucking know. Jesus. Those guys at the bar? I used to run with them."

"We figured that out," Cameron said. "We *were* there, you know."

I'd been so focused on Meadow, I hadn't really thought of it.

"So, you were a biker? I thought you were a hipster."

I looked at Dillon, who shrugged.

"Just trying to bring some levity to the situation, but I can tell that wasn't the right thing to say. So why don't you tell us what happened?"

Again, the kid was wise beyond his years. I didn't want to tell them any of this, but I owed it to them.

So I'd tell them everything. Well, mostly. Some things I didn't need to say. Ever.

Except to Meadow. If she asked, then I'd tell her.

"I used to be part of that club. I thought it was a family when I didn't have one of my own. My parents skipped town when I was young, and I finished high school but didn't do much after. You know, stupid shit."

"Considering that our lives were comprised of mostly stupid shit before we moved in with the Connollys, I get you," Aiden said dryly.

"Well, you ended up in a nice family. I ended up with a family that ran drugs."

"Really?" Dillon asked.

Suddenly, the kid sounded his age. Sure, he was nineteen now, but he was still so innocent in some ways. Of course, he had been through more shit than I had until I joined the club, so maybe he wasn't that innocent, after all.

"I didn't care about anyone's feelings. I did whatever I wanted. Did what I was told at the time when it came to the club business. Then they started moving into harsher things, and I didn't want to be a part of it anymore. I woke up with some girl in my lap that I didn't remember, the guys all laughing around me about some shit, and I walked away. They'd drugged me and I hadn't even known it had happened. They didn't let me walk away freely, though," I whispered.

I didn't need to tell them that part.

They could probably guess what had happened.

The movies weren't right, TV sure as hell wasn't, but there was still violence in my world. Scars on my back because of what they'd burned from my body.

I wished I could have been in one of the good clubs, but we were definitely one of the bad ones. One that gave the others a bad name.

"Anyway, I walked away with nothing but the clothes on my back and the bike under me. And I've been sort of on the run ever since. Because once you're in, you really don't get to leave. Not unless they want you to go."

"And you knew Meadow back then?" Aiden asked.

"I knew *of* her."

They looked at me as if waiting for more, but I wouldn't give it to them. Not when it wasn't my secret to tell.

"But, yeah, I didn't tell her where I came from or that I knew of her. So she didn't know that I knew anything. She's probably so fucking mad at me right now. She'll never want to talk with me again."

"And that's why she ran."

I looked at Brendon. "Yep. And I deserved that. I left the club because I had to. Because I didn't want to be the person I'd become. When I came here, I thought I could stay for a while. And then Meadow showed up. It was like a part of my past came back, and I was trying to figure out what to do with it. I tried to stay away. But I didn't. And now I don't know what to do."

"So you're just leaving?" Dillon asked, and I looked up at him.

"I think I have to."

"Will those guys come back?"

I shook my head. "No, I don't think so. Cliff doesn't have as much hold anymore after what he did. He had his group, but he was never the one who made decisions before. I figured that most of the guys knew where I was anyway. Knew I was out. And while I'll always be a traitor to them, they're not going to come and do anything violent to me."

"Didn't look like that last night," Aiden said.

"True. But that was only Cliff. Did you notice? Trace was the only one who said anything other than him. They just walked out. The bar should be safe. And I'll be okay. I hope." I wouldn't know for sure until something happened or didn't, but there was nothing I could do about that. I hadn't broken the law since I got out, and I wasn't going to do it again.

I wasn't a good person, or at least I hadn't been back then. And I had been trying to pay my penance ever since. Attempting to become a better man.

But I had still lied to Meadow.

"I don't know what I can say to Meadow. She wanted to be away from that, too. And I'm a constant reminder of what she left behind."

"You need to grovel," Dillon said, and we all looked at him.

I shook my head. "I can apologize, but I still need to keep away. I'm not good for her."

"Bullshit," Aiden said.

"Excuse me?" I asked.

"He's right. Bullshit," Cameron agreed. "You two are good for each other. You're not as much of a fucking asshole as you used to be. You laugh more, and you actually join us sometimes. And you brought Meadow out of her shell. I see the way you two look at each other. You guys are happy."

I just shook my head at Cameron.

"Maybe we were. But it was based on a lie."

"Then fix it," Dillon said.

"It's not that easy, kid."

"Nothing worth having is ever easy. All you guys taught me that. Hell, it's a saying for a reason."

"It might be a saying, but that doesn't mean it's a thing."

"Oh, shut up."

I stared at him.

"Find something worth fighting for. That's the whole point of this life of ours. We all came from shit. All of us. And we pulled through. You did. No, you didn't tell Meadow about your past. And that's on you. So…fix it. Apologize. Grovel. Grovel hard. But fix it. You're not going to know if she can forgive you unless you try. But if you walk away?

You'll likely hate yourself forever."

I just looked at him along with the others, and then Brendon shook his head and started laughing. "How the hell did you get to be so wise?" Brendon asked.

"I don't know. I listened to you guys, I guess. Sometimes you know what you're doing." The kid stuffed his hands into his pockets, and I rubbed my eyes.

"She's not going to forgive me."

"Like the kid said, you won't know until you try," Cameron whispered.

I looked at him and shrugged. "So I'm supposed to go to her and grovel, with no formal education, no job, and a past that is best left untold?"

"Well, first off, we're not all products of our pasts. We're allowed to have futures," Aiden said, holding up one finger. Then he held up another. "Second, you still have a job. Like I said, you don't get to quit."

"I was already part of a place that didn't let me quit," I said wryly.

"See? You can joke about it. You're fine."

I shook my head at Cameron. "Really?"

"No. But we're not going to fire you. We all have issues."

"Believe us. We all have issues," Brendon reiterated.

"I don't know what I'm doing," I whispered.

"None of us really do," Dillon said sagely.

I swear. That kid.

"I have no idea how to grovel," I said.

And then we all did the one thing we knew we could. We looked at Dillon. He rubbed his hands together and grinned.

"Okay, young padawans. Listen to Uncle Dillon. He'll explain."

Aiden snorted and smacked the kid upside the head playfully. Dillon beamed in response. I had a feeling that I was probably going to make another mistake. But doing what I did the way I did it had ruined everything. And the kid was right. I wouldn't know until I tried. And I really wanted to try.

Chapter 10

Beckham

I stood outside Meadow's door, hoping I was doing the right thing. I needed to apologize. I needed her to know that I was sorry. That I wished I had told her the truth. If she didn't take me back, if she didn't want me, I'd walk away. Because the error was on me.

And I had to be okay with that.

I had to be all right with walking away.

Even if I hated it.

The door opened before I could ring the bell, and she stood there, dark circles under her eyes and a shapeless sweatshirt over her body.

She looked beautiful. Stunning.

And I hoped to hell she forgave me. That she took me back. I just didn't know if she would.

"I saw you on the security cam. Figured I'd open the door before you stood here forever."

"I'm glad you have the security. It's good for you."

"I guess you knew the whole time why I have it. Didn't you?" she asked, a little sharpness in her tone.

I deserved that. And more.

"I want to apologize." I put my hands in my pockets as I looked at her, wanting to lower my shoulders so I didn't feel so big.

I knew what the club guys were like. What I had been like. No. I wasn't like them anymore. I had to remember that. And there had been worse.

Coby.

"Why don't you come in? No use standing out on the porch where everyone can see." She took a few steps in, and I followed her, hoping I'd figure out what to say.

I wasn't good at groveling. I had never done it before. But I would try.

"Why didn't you tell me?" she asked.

"Because I didn't know how." I sighed. "And because I was a coward. I should have told you right away that I knew who you were. But the thing was, I also wanted to know who you became. And that tripped me up. I'm sorry. I'll always be sorry for that. There aren't enough easy explanations to explain that away."

"I thought I had hidden it so well. Where I came from and all of that. Because I don't like the person I was back then." She looked at me, and I felt a kinship there. I only hoped it was enough.

"I didn't like the person I was either."

"I used to laugh at the girls who came in, wanting to be on a man's arm. Because I had mine. And that's what I was supposed to do—laugh and make fun of them and feel superior. I was a horrible person."

"I don't believe that."

She let out a laugh. "I wasn't the worst. I never hurt anyone. I was never cruel to their faces. But I wasn't the best person either. I've tried to be better since I left. I've tried to help anywhere I could. Bury who I became over time with the club. I thought I'd paid my penance for what I did."

She touched the scar on her wrist, and then I remembered. I recalled the scars on her hip, the ones on her ankle.

"I don't know everything, Meadow. I never did. Yes, I know who your dad is. And at one point, I knew you were with Coby. But I don't know it all. I was never one of those people laughing at you from behind your back. I never knew everything. I wanted you to tell me," I said softly.

"And you didn't. I thought it was all behind me. I didn't think I would ever have to think about it again. But then again, I didn't tell you anything either."

"If I had told you what I knew, then I would have had to tell you who I was. And I was ashamed of that."

"My parents practically sold me to Coby," she muttered.

My hands fisted at my sides, and I growled. "I figured. That's how the clubs do things."

"Well, it didn't really work out. I got away. You saw the scars. You know who Coby was. What he was like."

"And if I could strangle him right now, I would."

"It wouldn't be enough. But he's in my past. And I've worked with therapists over the years to try and figure out exactly who I am. I'm not just a broken shell. I'm not the person I was. Yes, I'm quiet, but that's because I think about what to say and how I need to be the person I am, rather than the person I was. I have all the locks and the security that I can get, but I'm not as scared as I used to be. I'm not that person anymore."

I took a step forward unconsciously, and she didn't pull away. I was grateful. "I'm not the same person either."

"Will you tell me who you were?"

And so I did. I told her how I joined the club, the things I did. I told her how I left. Explained the real story behind the scars on my back. I told her everything. And then she told me about Coby. About what he had done to her, what her parents still did.

And as I watched tears fall down her face, I held everything in so I wouldn't punch something. So I wouldn't scream in rage at my lack of control. There was nothing I could do. All I could do was listen and hope to hell that she would be okay. I didn't think she could forgive me. I didn't think she could look at me like she had before.

I was a reminder of a past she had tried to run from.

Like she was *my* reminder.

And while I knew I wanted her at my side forever, I wasn't sure if she wanted the same from me.

"I don't know what to do now," she whispered.

And then I remembered that I hadn't done the one thing I should. What Dillon had told me to do. Grovel. So, I went down to my knees in front of her.

Her eyes widened, and she looked at me like I was crazy.

"I'm sorry. I'm so damn sorry. I'm sorry I didn't stay in long enough to see what Coby became. I'm sorry I couldn't save you from him."

"That was never on your shoulders. Never your burden."

She reached out, tracing my brow with her fingertips.

I closed my eyes and barely resisted the urge to lean in to her touch.

"But because I knew your dad, and I knew of you through him, I stayed away. I knew I needed to keep my distance."

"But then you asked me to dance," she whispered.

I nodded. "And it was the best moment of my life. I'm sorry I didn't stay away."

"I'm sorry I couldn't do the same."

I closed my eyes, holding back everything so I could breathe and focus. "We're out, though, babe. And we're always going to be."

She looked at me then, her eyes wide.

"We're not those people anymore. We're allowed to move on and have a future. I want to know you. The person in front of me. I want to test the path we could have together. I want to figure out what this thing between us could be. Please, forgive me. Know that no matter what happens, I'm not the person I was before. I tried to atone for my sins, attempted to find the path that led to a salvation that I knew would never truly come. But in my heart, I hope that you're on that road with me. Maybe not on the bike behind me because riding is such a different thing, but perhaps holding my hand as I try to figure things out."

I snorted as I finished, shaking my head as she stood there staring.

"I was never good with poetry. But just know that I fell for you when I held you that first time. When you wore that green dress that made your eyes shine. I fell in love with you when you said yes to my request to dance, and even more when I had my lips on yours for the first time. And I'm going to love you for the rest of my life. I'll never forgive myself for hurting you, for bringing back the past. But I know that if we try, we have a chance. There can be a future where it's not about where we came from, or the sins we committed. But rather what we can do to atone for them. I hope you'll be by my side as we do it. I hope you'll forgive me."

She was quiet for so long that I had to wonder what to do. Did I get up off my knees and walk out? Did I keep speaking? Or did I remain kneeling and stay silent?

Her hands caressed my face, and a single tear fell down her cheek.

"I didn't know you before. But I know you now. And I think…I think we can try."

My heart burst open, hope and pain radiating through me and twirling around like a tornado.

I could hardly breathe, barely comprehend what she'd said. Nothing had ever felt like this before. And there were no blueprints. No roadmaps for me to figure out what to say or what to do.

"I fell for you then, too. Or maybe it was when you smiled at me from behind the bar. Or when you touched my jaw to see if I was okay. I want to know who you are, too. I want to find that peace and figure out what to do. I don't want to think about where we came from. I just want to move on. I want to figure out who we are now. And there's nothing to forgive, Beckham. We both have our faults. It's what we do with our lives now that matters."

I pulled her close, put my hand on the back of her head, and tugged her lips to mine.

And when she succumbed, kissing me back, I knew that we could do this. This was the moment we would start again.

I had been taken with her all along, since the first moment I met her.

When we were two separate journeys intertwined.

We would have to figure things out, and there would be more bumps in our road.

But as she kissed me, I knew we could weather the storm.

We had each other. I had her.

The girl in the green dress with the wide eyes.

She was mine.

Epilogue

I found my perfection. Him.
No, he's not perfect. Nor am I.
But we can find our own way.
~Meadow, journal entry

Meadow

"Touch yourself," he commanded, and I obeyed, arching my back as I slowly slipped my hands up my body to cup my breasts. I rolled my nipples between my fingers, my eyes on his as he slowly worked his cock in and out of me.

"More," I whispered.

I needed more.

He grinned, his hands on my hips as he continued to work his dick in and out of my tight sheath.

"We're going to break your table if I go any harder," he drawled, and I grinned harder, slowly playing with my nipples.

He loved when I touched myself, just like I loved when he did the same. The day before, I had been in the shower, getting myself off with my showerhead as he stood outside the door, working himself with his hand. We had both come, calling out each other's names, and then he was down on his knees as the water cooled around us, getting me off once again with his mouth.

His beard between my thighs was the best sensation ever. I was a very wicked woman. And I loved every minute of it.

"I can get a new table," I panted, letting go of my breasts. I reached out, slamming my hands down on his chest, though it wasn't easy since he was too far away from me to really grab on to.

"Beckham," I whispered. "Please."

He leaned over me, a smirk reaching his eyes. I loved when he looked at me like that. It was so sexy, even though it shouldn't be. On anyone else, it would be a horrible thing that would make me roll my eyes and walk away. Prove the size of their ego. On him? It was perfect.

"Okay, cupcake. You asked for it."

He thrust once, hard, and I groaned. "Don't"—thrust—"call"—thrust—"me"—another thrust—"cupcake."

He stilled and then moved faster. His lips were on mine, my hands on his back as he slowly worked in and out of me before going faster and reaching a crescendo that sent us both over the edge. The table made a pained noise, and I winced as it shook beneath us. When one table leg creaked so loudly I was afraid it might snap, I pushed him off me, even as he kept moving. He simply rolled his eyes, gripped my hips, and somehow lifted me while continuing to thrust.

The strength of the man almost made me come immediately.

But I held on, gripping his shoulders as he pumped in and out of me as fast as he could, even as we were standing. When I slid one hand between us, slowly flicking my clit, he grunted, coming inside me as I clamped his dick with my orgasm.

"Jesus Christ," he mumbled, and I laughed.

"Well, I guess you were right about the table." He squeezed my ass with one hand and slapped my hip with the other.

"We were going to break it one day," he said before slowly sliding out of me.

He reached for a towel and cleaned us up, and then I stood beside him in my kitchen, shaking my head.

"I probably do need a new table."

"Before you get one, we'll make sure we break this one in just right."

"By 'break in,' you mean break completely?"

"Probably. You doing okay, cupcake?"

I reached between us and squeezed his balls until his eyes crossed.

"What did I say about calling me cupcake?"

"That I shouldn't? I don't know. I like it when you get all fiery and feisty on me. It's kind of a turn-on."

"We are late for dinner with our friends. You know Brendon's working the bar, and you can't mock him if you aren't there."

His eyebrows shot up, and I laughed.

"I know that's your favorite pastime."

"I'll have you know we were just engaged in my favorite pastime."

I laughed at him, then went up on my tiptoes so I could kiss his bearded chin before running off to the bathroom so I could finish getting ready.

He chased me but, thankfully, I closed the door in his face so he couldn't delay me any more.

"You're a cruel, cruel woman," he called from the other side of the door.

"You have stuff in the other bathroom. Use it."

I didn't mention that I wanted him to move in completely. We weren't ready for that. We were getting closer, but ever since we'd found out that our paths were connected, we had tried to start at square one. Not that we'd ever had a square one. But we were taking things slowly, even if that meant having sex on my dining room table where it could break at any moment.

I smiled at that, then went and showered before getting ready as quickly as I could.

Beckham was waiting for me in the living room when I walked out, and he stood up abruptly from the couch before coming over to kiss me hard on the mouth.

"You ready to go mock Brendon?" he asked, and I laughed.

"You're the one who mocks. I try to hold him back from beating your ass."

"He could try," Beckham said with a laugh, and I shook my head in response as we turned off all the lights and headed to the bar.

We hadn't heard from anyone from either of the clubs since that night a few months ago. My mom would probably call again eventually, just to annoy me. And I honestly didn't know what I would say. But I knew that, no matter what, I wouldn't be going back. They weren't after me. Coby would be behind bars for a good long while. At least, that's what I hoped. No more appeals for him. Nobody from the club wanted Beckham back in. Nobody wanted me back. And while we would always be careful, we had a future with each other. And that's what I had to remember. We might be the products of our mistakes, but that wasn't the end game. We had more to give.

And as I walked into the bar with the love of my life on my arm, I knew that I had found my peace. Even in the place I hadn't been looking, the exact opposite of where I thought I'd find it.

Aiden and Sienna were off in a corner, yelling at one another even as they laughed and joked. They were probably fighting over food or one of their many cats. I loved the way they acted with each other. Violet and Cameron were already in the booth, having a talk with Dillon and Dillon's latest girlfriend. I wasn't sure what number this was, but apparently, college life was good for the kid. He was always respectful, but there was no chance that the romantic at heart would be settling down anytime soon.

Watching Cameron and Violet fall for each other during the worst times of their lives had been beautiful even as it had been painful. One day, watching Dillon fall in love would be wonderful, too. I couldn't wait for it to happen.

I squeezed Beckham's hand as we walked over to the bar, Harmony and Brendon behind the counter, laughing at each other as they worked.

I slowly put my hand over Beckham's mouth before he could say anything, and he kissed my fingertips.

"Be nice," I whispered.

"I'm always nice."

I raised a brow. No, he wasn't. But then again, I hadn't always been either.

But these people that had made us their family meant everything to me. Harmony had been given her second chance.

I was coming to realize that maybe we were allowed more than one chance at happiness. And the man at my side was mine.

We all came from different backgrounds, and with varied connections, and even though Beckham and I had once been fractured, we were slowly putting ourselves back together.

The Connollys had taken us in, even knowing we came from dark places. But then again, so had they.

These people were my peace, my future.

And as I held onto Beckham's side, laughing at something Brendon said, I had to remember that this was where the future lay.

No past was required.

I had been taken with him from the first moment I saw him, and that was something I would never forget.

No past was needed. Only a future paved with our own choices.

* * * *

Also from 1001 Dark Nights and Carrie Ann Ryan, discover Ashes to Ink, Inked Nights, Wicked Wolf, Hidden Ink, and Adoring Ink.

Sign up for the 1001 Dark Nights Newsletter
and be entered to win a Tiffany Key necklace.

There's a contest every month!

To subscribe, go to www.1001DarkNights.com.

**As a bonus, all subscribers can download
FIVE FREE exclusive books!**

Discover 1001 Dark Nights Collection Seven

For more information, visit www.1001DarkNights.com.

THE BISHOP by Skye Warren
A Tanglewood Novella

TAKEN WITH YOU by Carrie Ann Ryan
A Fractured Connections Novella

DRAGON LOST by Donna Grant
A Dark Kings Novella

SEXY LOVE by Carly Phillips
A Sexy Series Novella

PROVOKE by Rachel Van Dyken
A Seaside Pictures Novella

RAFE by Sawyer Bennett
An Arizona Vengeance Novella

THE NAUGHTY PRINCESS by Claire Contreras
A Sexy Royals Novella

THE GRAVEYARD SHIFT by Darynda Jones
A Charley Davidson Novella

CHARMED by Lexi Blake
A Masters and Mercenaries Novella

SACRIFICE OF DARKNESS by Alexandra Ivy
A Guardians of Eternity Novella

THE QUEEN by Jen Armentrout
A Wicked Novella

BEGIN AGAIN by Jennifer Probst
A Stay Novella

VIXEN by Rebecca Zanetti
A Dark Protectors/Rebels Novella

SLASH by Laurelin Paige
A Slay Series Novella

THE DEAD HEAT OF SUMMER by Heather Graham
A Krewe of Hunters Novella

WILD FIRE by Kristen Ashley
A Chaos Novella

MORE THAN PROTECT YOU by Shayla Black
A More Than Words Novella

LOVE SONG by Kylie Scott
A Stage Dive Novella

CHERISH ME by J. Kenner
A Stark Ever After Novella

SHINE WITH ME by Kristen Proby
A With Me in Seattle Novella

And new from Blue Box Press:

TEASE ME by J. Kenner
A Stark International Novel

Discover More Carrie Ann Ryan

Ashes to Ink
A Montgomery Ink: Colorado Springs Novella

Back in Denver, Abby lost everything she ever loved, except for her daughter, the one memory she has left of the man she loved and lost. Now, she's moved next to the Montgomerys in Colorado Springs, leaving her past behind to start her new life.

One step at a time.

Ryan is the newest tattoo artist at Montgomery Ink Too and knows the others are curious about his secrets. But he's not ready to tell them. Not yet. That is…until he meets Abby.

Abby and Ryan thought they had their own paths, ones that had nothing to do with one another. Then…they took a chance.

On each other.

One night at a time.

* * * *

Inked Nights
A Montgomery Ink Novella

Tattoo artist, Derek Hawkins knows the rules:
  One night a month.
  No last names.
  No promises.

Olivia Madison has her own rules:
  Don't fall in love.
  No commitment.
  Never tell Derek the truth.

When their worlds crash into each other however, Derek and Olivia will have to face what they fought to ignore as well as the connection they tried to forget.

Adoring Ink
A Montgomery Ink Novella

Holly Rose fell in love with a Montgomery, but left him when he couldn't love her back. She might have been the one to break the ties and ensure her ex's happy ending, but now Holly's afraid she's missed out on more than a chance at forever. Though she's always been the dependable good girl, she's ready to take a leap of faith and embark on the journey of a lifetime.

Brody Deacon loves ink, women, fast cars, and living life like there's no tomorrow. The thing is, he doesn't know if he *has* a tomorrow at all. When he sees Holly, he's not only intrigued, he also hears the warnings of danger in his head. She's too sweet, too innocent, and way too special for him. But when Holly asks him to help her grab the bull by the horns, he can't help but go all in.

As they explore Holly's bucket list and their own desires, Brody will have to make sure he doesn't fall too hard and too fast. Sometimes, people think happily ever afters don't happen for everyone, and Brody will have to face his demons and tell Holly the truth of what it means to truly live life to the fullest…even when they're both running out of time.

Hidden Ink
A Montgomery Ink Novella

The Montgomery Ink series continues with the long-awaited romance between the café owner next door and the tattoo artist who's loved her from afar.

Hailey Monroe knows the world isn't always fair, but she's picked herself up from the ashes once before and if she needs to, she'll do it again. It's been years since she first spotted the tattoo artist with a scowl that made her heart skip a beat, but now she's finally gained the courage to approach him. Only it won't be about what their future could bring, but how to finish healing the scars from her past.

Sloane Gordon lived through the worst kinds of hell yet the temptation next door sends him to another level. He's kept his distance because he knows what kind of man he is versus what kind of man Hailey needs. When she comes to him with a proposition that sends his mind whirling and his soul shattering, he'll do everything in his power to protect the woman he cares for and the secrets he's been forced to keep.

* * * *

Wicked Wolf
A Redwood Pack Novella

The war between the Redwood Pack and the Centrals is one of wolf legend. Gina Eaton lost both of her parents when a member of their Pack betrayed them. Adopted by the Alpha of the Pack as a child, Gina grew up within the royal family to become an enforcer and protector of her den. She's always known fate can be a tricky and deceitful entity, but when she finds the one man that could be her mate, she might throw caution to the wind and follow the path set out for her, rather than forging one of her own.

Quinn Weston's mate walked out on him five years ago, severing their bond in the most brutal fashion. She not only left him a shattered shadow of himself, but their newborn son as well. Now, as the lieutenant of the Talon Pack's Alpha, he puts his whole being into two things: the safety of his Pack and his son.

When the two Alphas put Gina and Quinn together to find a way to ensure their treaties remain strong, fate has a plan of its own. Neither knows what will come of the Pack's alliance, let alone one between the two of them. The past paved their paths in blood and heartache, but it will take the strength of a promise and iron will to find their future.

Wrapped in Ink

Montgomery Ink: Boulder Book 1
By Carrie Ann Ryan
Now Available

The Montgomery Ink saga continues with a new series set in Boulder, where a family secret might just change everything.

One mistake at a friend's wedding rocks Liam Montgomery's entire world, and everything he thought was true turns out to be a lie. But when an accident lands him in the ER, Liam meets someone that might just be the distraction he needs.

Arden Brady has spent her life in and out of hospitals. But according to the world, she doesn't look sick. She's lost jobs and friends because they don't see beneath the surface, but she's learned to rely on her family and herself to keep going. And then she meets Liam.

With two sets of overprotective siblings and a puppy that can't help but get into everything, Liam and Arden might just fall harder than either one ever expected.

* * * *

Chapter One

Liam Montgomery leaned against the wall and did his best to stay out of the way. It wasn't easy since, like the rest of his family, he was broad and tall and tended to stand out amongst the crowd—that is, unless the crowd was full of Montgomerys. Then, he blended in.

Today, however, only a fraction of the Montgomerys were here—his immediate family—and not what felt like tens of thousands of cousins, uncles, and aunts that lived in the state.

Liam looked over the crush of wedding goers as they milled around with their pre-ceremony drinks and tried to spot his family. The Boulder Montgomerys had been invited to his friends' wedding and had all shown up, which was nice, considering that though they all lived in the same city, they were rarely in the same place unless there was a family dinner.

Those didn't come often these days since they were all busier than usual, but Liam had a feeling that once his mom saw all her ducklings in one place, there would be an edict for a dinner sometime soon.

Liam sipped the last of his beer and then looked around for a tray to set it down on since he was finished. He nodded at an attendant as they took his bottle and then leaned back against the wall. He never really understood why someone needed a drink before a wedding unless you were the one getting married, but he didn't really mind that he could have a beer while waiting for everything to start.

"Why are you over here sulking?" Bristol asked as she came to his side and leaned into him. Liam wrapped his arms around his little sister's shoulders and kissed the top of her head. She let out a strangled noise, and he knew that she was rolling her eyes at him even though he couldn't see her face just then.

"Really? Really?" She sounded so annoyed that Liam couldn't help but grin.

He turned to face her. "What? You're my baby sister. I'm allowed to do things like that." He reached out to mess with her hair again, and she pulled away, huffing.

"I'm in my thirties. You don't have to coddle me and kiss me on the top of the head like I'm still wearing braids."

Liam narrowed his eyes and then traced his finger along one of the tiny braids in her updo. "Um, I beg to differ with the whole braids thing."

She glared at him and then flipped him off. "It's two tiny little braids in my updo that the hairstylist had fun with. I'm not actually in pigtails. Stop treating me like a baby."

"I'm always going to treat you like a baby. Because you're my baby sister."

"You don't treat Aaron like you do me, and he's younger than I am."

"He might be, and I do treat him like a baby brother. But you're still the wee little girl."

She flipped him off and then winced as their parents' voices hit them. "Did I just see you flipping off your brother at a very fancy event?" Francine Montgomery asked as she came up to stand by them, tapping her daughter on the nose.

"Surely, we did not," Timothy Montgomery asserted, holding back a grin.

Considering that both of Liam's parents flipped each other off constantly, as did the rest of the Montgomery family, Liam knew that it was all bluster. But mothering Bristol or any of them was sort of what their mom did. And he knew she loved it.

"Liam started it," Bristol said, and Liam burst out laughing.

"Oh, yes, that's the mature sister I know and love," he added as Bristol punched him in the gut.

He let out an *oof* and rubbed his stomach.

"You're packing a punch there, baby sister," he muttered.

Bristol coughed and used her hands to cover up the middle finger she used to flip him off with again.

"I still saw that, young lady. And you shouldn't hit your brother like that," their mother added. Liam just shook his head.

He loved his family, he really did. But, sometimes, it felt like they were in their own little comedy show outside of the world, a place where nothing mattered but them. And he was fine with that. They had always been there for him. They were the true friends and close relatives he'd had all his life.

Liam was a Montgomery, just like the rest of them. They had connections and ties that never died, no matter how much they made fun of each other or flipped each other off. Because they were family, and that's what mattered most.

As his brothers came walking in, grinning at him and Bristol, Liam leaned back against the wall and looked at them all.

Ethan was only a couple of years younger than Liam and brilliant. He didn't understand half the things that Ethan talked about when he spoke about his job, but that didn't matter. His brother was just that damn good at everything.

And Aaron? Aaron was brilliant in his own way. He might not be science and math smart like Ethan, but the art that he created was breathtaking, and Liam knew it would last into the ages.

Just like Bristol's music would.

They were all so damn talented and amazing. And while he sometimes felt a little left behind, he knew he shouldn't. Because he liked his job, and he was damn good at it. He'd even liked it when he was a model back in the day, even though everyone had made fun of him for it.

But it had made him enough money to get him through college. With some left over to help the rest of his family so nobody ended up in debt.

If he had to deal with being called "pretty boy" and made fun of for his looks? He'd take it.

And he'd flip off his family as he did.

"What are we doing over here?" Aaron asked, frowning. "Is there some kind of Montgomery reunion I wasn't aware of?"

"I'm just so happy that all of our family is together in one place," Francine said, sliding in between Liam's two brothers and wrapping her arms around their waists. "Y'all are getting so big."

Liam snorted. "Um, Mom? I think we've all gone way past the whole growing up stage. We're pretty much as big as we're gonna get."

"I don't know, Liam, I think Bristol might one day actually grow up and reach normal height at some point." Ethan winked and patted Bristol on the head.

Their baby sister narrowed her eyes and used both fingers this time, raising them high into the air. She quickly lowered them as Francine and Timothy glared at her.

"At least *try* to act like we're not all heathens," Timothy said, although he laughed as he did. "We're supposed to be the nice family at a beautiful wedding, not people flipping each other off just because we can. It gets kind of old after a while."

"That is true," Liam added. He was surprised that Bristol didn't flip him off again.

"If everyone would stop touching my hair, though, that would be amazing," Bristol added.

"Your hair does look lovely, dear," Francine said, studying her daughter. "Did Zia do it?"

Liam met his brothers' gazes and held back a grin.

It didn't matter how long Zia and Bristol had been broken up, their mother wanted marriages for her children. And babies. And so, the fact that Bristol and her ex-girlfriend were still friends always gave Francine hope.

Besides, it took the attention off the rest of them so they weren't constantly being asked when they were going to settle down and find a nice boy or girl to marry. Liam wasn't ready for that, and after he had witnessed all the trouble and heartache that his cousins had gone through in their marriages, he was okay waiting that out for a little while. He had time. Lots of time.

The fact that he was thinking all of this at his friends' wedding wasn't lost on him. Craig and Cain had been through their own hells, but were now going to say their vows to each other and then head off into the sunset, happily married. Maybe they'd eventually adopt a baby because they were on the right path for that.

Liam was fine on his own road, thank you very much.

"Zia didn't do my hair, Mom," Bristol said, and Liam knew she was holding back a sigh. "She's not even in town."

"But did she help you with the style or something? She's just so amazing with all her techniques and things. I follow her on Instagram, you know? She's getting her own makeup line and everything. Did you know that, Bristol?"

Zia was an Instagram beauty blogger who was getting her own product line or something like that. Liam was the one who had introduced her to Bristol since he used to model with her back in the day. It was still a little weird to think that his baby sister had exes in her life. He tried not to think of Bristol as someone who could actually have a relationship. But Zia had been good. Not right for Bristol, but good.

"I know, Mom. Zia and her boyfriend are out of town on vacation, though." Bristol emphasized the word *boyfriend*, and their mother's face fell.

"Oh, I didn't know she was seeing someone."

"Has been for a few months now. I think I hear wedding bells."

"Speaking of wedding bells," Ethan put in. "We should probably find our seats, or Craig and Cain will beat the crap out of us for ruining their wedding."

"Yeah, we can't ruin another one," Aaron put in and then laughed.

"What wedding have we ruined?"

"I'm sure we ruined a few," Aaron put in, waving his hand.

Liam laughed and put his arms around Bristol's shoulders as they all walked into the seating area. "I'm sure our mere presence does that. They can't help but be intimidated by us. We are the Montgomerys, after all."

"They're probably just intimidated by you, pretty boy," Ethan said, ducking out of the way as Liam tried to punch him.

"Boys," their mom said in that voice that had been the same since they were little. One word and they all stopped.

Even Bristol froze.

"Sorry," they all mumbled under their breaths and then looked at each other, grinning.

No, they weren't kids anymore, nowhere close, actually, but sometimes, it was good to be near family. Liam took a seat at the end of the bench with Bristol sitting next to him, and then Ethan, Aaron, and their parents. Liam had met Cain back in his modeling days, and the two of them had struck up a friendship that had lasted through the years.

Yeah, Liam had been a teenage model, and it continued into his twenties. He'd made a shit ton of money but then left that life as quickly as he could. Somehow, he hadn't found his way into drugs or too much drinking or getting a disease from all the women he could have slept with over that time. A few of his friends back in the day had succumbed to exactly that. It didn't matter what decade you were in, it felt like the craze of wanting to do something bad and be in that circle just kept coming at you.

Liam had then met Craig in his *new* job. Liam had been at his agency in New York, meeting his representative for a new book deal when Craig had come out, muttering about authors and lattes and something else. Craig had been an intern at the time and was now a full-time editor at Liam's publishing house—not *his* editor since Maisie would never let him go. Liam had struck up a conversation with Craig when they were both waiting for a meeting.

Then he'd introduced Craig to Cain, and the two of them had hit it off.

They'd also come to visit Liam enough times in Colorado that they had finally bought another home in the Rockies.

And so, they'd decided to get married and have their ceremony in the mountains of Boulder, rather than in the city on the east coast.

Liam figured that the couple would probably have another party out in New York, but that was fine with him. He might just hop on a plane and fly out there for that, too. He liked the two grooms, and they deserved this and much more.

However, the way his mother kept looking around at all the wedding decorations and everything else, he had a feeling that this was simply one more nail in the coffin of his bachelorhood.

Not that he was actively against getting married, he just hadn't found the right person yet. None of the Montgomerys in this city had.

But his mother was determined to have her way and make sure that the wedding bells never ceased.

A Montgomery wedding was what she wanted. And, apparently, it was what she was going to get, no matter the cost.

At least that's what she had said at their last family dinner, causing his siblings and him to burst out laughing.

It was like she was waging war, and weddings and babies were the only way to end it.

Well, she'd have to wait a bit longer. Because today was about Craig and Cain, not the Montgomerys. Even if it felt like they were the center of their own world sometimes.

The music started, and Liam just leaned back onto the bench and looked around. They were outdoors, the sun shining, and the mountains gleaming against the blue sky. Didn't matter what season it was, even if it was freezing outside, the sky could still be blue. And then he figured that a snowstorm or a thunderstorm would likely come out of nowhere and drench everyone, but they had these few precious moments. And they were going to take them.

Craig and Cain looked hot as hell in their matching tuxes and grins. Liam shook his head when Cain dipped Craig into a very intense, very not-wedding-like kiss.

There were hoots and hollers, mostly by him and his brothers, and Bristol wiped her tears, laughed, and looked on with the rest of the crowd as the two men began the next phase of their lives together.

"That was so beautiful," Francine said, wiping her face. "I just can't wait to see what happens at your weddings."

"Mom," Liam sighed.

"What? I have four beautiful children, and none of them want to be married. None of you are actually in relationships. What have I done wrong?"

"Do you ever feel like she was born in the wrong century?" Bristol asked, tapping her chin.

"You mean that she's like a Regency momma, watching her little ducklings not able to find their duke or their lord at a ballroom?" Ethan asked.

"Yes, I think we're all wallflowers here," Bristol said, sounding so serious that he almost thought she meant it. Then he looked in her eyes and saw the laughter.

"There's nothing wallflower about you, Bristol."

"Oh, that's so sweet. Seriously. But again, I don't really want to get married right now. You know, I would kind of need a boyfriend or a girlfriend to make that happen."

"Well, don't say that too loudly, or you know Mom will just fly someone out to find you." Ethan shook his head and grinned. "I swear she's going to start setting us up on blind dates or bringing people to family dinners if we don't start pairing off soon."

"That may be true, but Bristol would be first, right?" Liam asked quickly.

"Oh, no. I'm not going first. You're the eldest. You're the one who gets to get married."

"No, don't the dukes and the sons of dukes get to wait until their little baby sister is presented for her opening and pushed out into the real world without a net?" Liam asked and then paused. "Is the word opening? What is the word?"

"Debut," Aaron said, and everybody looked at him. "What? I happen to know a few women who read historical romance."

They all *kept* looking.

"Okay, just because Lisa Kleypas is one of my favorite authors does not mean I lose my man card."

They all started laughing, and Bristol hugged Aaron hard.

"I think that makes you the best. Because her Wallflower series is seriously one of my favorites ever."

"I know, right?" Aaron asked. Liam just looked at Ethan before they both cracked up laughing.

It was good to be with the family. Good to be smiling and acting as if they all weren't sometimes stressed with their jobs or the fact that their mom really wanted them to settle down. It was good not to think about anything but being with the people that mattered the most. His family.

The four of them stood off to the side near the outside of the building where there was some restoration work being done, trying to stay out of the way. They tended to be loud, and this was about Craig and Cain and their day, so none of them really wanted to be the center of attention.

Nor did they want to be near the group when ties and garters were being thrown in place of bouquets.

Liam knew that his mother was probably hunting for them since the time for the toss was almost upon them, so they were hiding.

A little.

Liam looked up when he heard a scratching sound and frowned. "What was that?" he said, his voice soft.

"What was what?" Bristol asked, and then her eyes widened.

"Liam!"

Liam looked to the right and then threw himself over his little sister as the scaffolding that had been right beside them fell. There was a sharp pain, and a deafening crunch as he heard his little sister scream, his brothers shout to him, and then he heard no more.

There was only darkness.

Nothing.

About Carrie Ann Ryan

Carrie Ann Ryan is the *New York Times* and *USA Today* bestselling author of contemporary, paranormal, and young adult romance. Her works include the Montgomery Ink, Redwood Pack, Fractured Connections, and Elements of Five series, which have sold over 3.0 million books worldwide. She started writing while in graduate school for her advanced degree in chemistry and hasn't stopped since. Carrie Ann has written over seventy-five novels and novellas with more in the works. When she's not losing herself in her emotional and action-packed worlds, she's reading as much as she can while wrangling her clowder of cats who have more followers than she does.

www.CarrieAnnRyan.com

Discover 1001 Dark Nights

For more information, visit www.1001DarkNights.com.

COLLECTION THREE
HIDDEN INK by Carrie Ann Ryan
BLOOD ON THE BAYOU by Heather Graham
SEARCHING FOR MINE by Jennifer Probst
DANCE OF DESIRE by Christopher Rice
ROUGH RHYTHM by Tessa Bailey
DEVOTED by Lexi Blake
Z by Larissa Ione
FALLING UNDER YOU by Laurelin Paige
EASY FOR KEEPS by Kristen Proby
UNCHAINED by Elisabeth Naughton
HARD TO SERVE by Laura Kaye
DRAGON FEVER by Donna Grant
KAYDEN/SIMON by Alexandra Ivy/Laura Wright
STRUNG UP by Lorelei James
MIDNIGHT UNTAMED by Lara Adrian
TRICKED by Rebecca Zanetti
DIRTY WICKED by Shayla Black
THE ONLY ONE by Lauren Blakely
SWEET SURRENDER by Liliana Hart

COLLECTION FOUR
ROCK CHICK REAWAKENING by Kristen Ashley
ADORING INK by Carrie Ann Ryan
SWEET RIVALRY by K. Bromberg
SHADE'S LADY by Joanna Wylde
RAZR by Larissa Ione
ARRANGED by Lexi Blake
TANGLED by Rebecca Zanetti
HOLD ME by J. Kenner
SOMEHOW, SOME WAY by Jennifer Probst
TOO CLOSE TO CALL by Tessa Bailey
HUNTED by Elisabeth Naughton
EYES ON YOU by Laura Kaye
BLADE by Alexandra Ivy/Laura Wright
DRAGON BURN by Donna Grant
TRIPPED OUT by Lorelei James
STUD FINDER by Lauren Blakely
MIDNIGHT UNLEASHED by Lara Adrian

HALLOW BE THE HAUNT by Heather Graham
DIRTY FILTHY FIX by Laurelin Paige
THE BED MATE by Kendall Ryan
NIGHT GAMES by CD Reiss
NO RESERVATIONS by Kristen Proby
DAWN OF SURRENDER by Liliana Hart

COLLECTION FIVE
BLAZE ERUPTING by Rebecca Zanetti
ROUGH RIDE by Kristen Ashley
HAWKYN by Larissa Ione
RIDE DIRTY by Laura Kaye
ROME'S CHANCE by Joanna Wylde
THE MARRIAGE ARRANGEMENT by Jennifer Probst
SURRENDER by Elisabeth Naughton
INKED NIGHTS by Carrie Ann Ryan
ENVY by Rachel Van Dyken
PROTECTED by Lexi Blake
THE PRINCE by Jennifer L. Armentrout
PLEASE ME by J. Kenner
WOUND TIGHT by Lorelei James
STRONG by Kylie Scott
DRAGON NIGHT by Donna Grant
TEMPTING BROOKE by Kristen Proby
HAUNTED BE THE HOLIDAYS by Heather Graham
CONTROL by K. Bromberg
HUNKY HEARTBREAKER by Kendall Ryan
THE DARKEST CAPTIVE by Gena Showalter

COLLECTION SIX

DRAGON CLAIMED by Donna Grant
ASHES TO INK by Carrie Ann Ryan
ENSNARED by Elisabeth Naughton
EVERMORE by Corinne Michaels
VENGEANCE by Rebecca Zanetti
ELI'S TRIUMPH by Joanna Wylde
CIPHER by Larissa Ione
RESCUING MACIE by Susan Stoker

ENCHANTED by Lexi Blake
TAKE THE BRIDE by Carly Phillips
INDULGE ME by J. Kenner
THE KING by Jennifer L. Armentrout
QUIET MAN by Kristen Ashley
ABANDON by Rachel Van Dyken
THE OPEN DOOR by Laurelin Paige
CLOSER by Kylie Scott
SOMETHING JUST LIKE THIS by Jennifer Probst
BLOOD NIGHT by Heather Graham
TWIST OF FATE by Jill Shalvis
MORE THAN PLEASURE YOU by Shayla Black
WONDER WITH ME by Kristen Proby
THE DARKEST ASSASSIN by Gena Showalter

Discover Blue Box Press

TAME ME by J. Kenner
TEMPT ME by J. Kenner
DAMIEN by J. Kenner
TEASE ME by J. Kenner
REAPER by Larissa Ione
THE SURRENDER GATE by Christopher Rice
SERVICING THE TARGET by Cherise Sinclair

On Behalf of 1001 Dark Nights,

Liz Berry, M.J. Rose, and Jillian Stein would like to thank ~

Steve Berry
Doug Scofield
Benjamin Stein
Kim Guidroz
InkSlinger PR
Dan Slater
Asha Hossain
Chris Graham
Chelle Olson
Kasi Alexander
Jessica Johns
Dylan Stockton
Richard Blake
and Simon Lipskar

Made in the USA
Coppell, TX
24 January 2020